Dear Reader,

Years ago while visiting D——, ————, I was sitting on the beach when a little girl strolled by. She looked lost and I was just about to offer her help when a man came rushing up, swooping her into his arms. The child squealed. For a moment, I panicked. But I quickly saw that she was screeching with glee. She was so happy that her daddy had found her!

Long after they had disappeared, I found myself thinking about the incident. What would I have done had the little girl cried and acted frightened of the man? Would I have had the courage to approach him had I suspected that he was intending to kidnap the child? And if I were to prevent an abduction, how might that impact my life?

These questions were the "seeds" that sprouted *Fortune's Bride*. I hope you enjoy my story.

Donna Clayton

DONNA CLAYTON

is the recipient of the Diamond Author Award For Literary Achievement 2000 as well as two HOLT Medallions. She became a writer through her love of reading. As a child, she marveled at the ability to travel the world, experience swash-buckling adventures and meet amazingly bold and daring people without ever leaving the shade of the huge oak in her very own backyard. This love of reading sparked in her a passion for creating "flesh-and-blood" characters and story lines that enable them to learn and grow and open their hearts to love. In her opinion, love *is* what makes the world go 'round. She takes great pride in knowing that, through her work, she provides her readers the chance to indulge in some purely selfish romantic entertainment.

One of her favorite pastimes is traveling. Her other interests include walking, reading, visiting with friends, teaching Sunday school, cooking and baking, and she still collects cookbooks, too. In fact, her house is overrun with them.

Please write to Donna care of Silhouette Books. She'd love to hear from you!

Books by Donna Clayton

Silhouette Romance

Mountain Laurel #720
Taking Love in Stride #781
Return of the Runaway Bride #999
Wife for a While #1039
Nanny and the Professor #1066
Fortune's Bride #1118
Daddy Down the Aisle #1162
*Miss Maxwell Becomes a Mom #1211
*Nanny in the Nick of Time #1217
*Beauty and the Bachelor Dad #1223
†The Stand-By Significant Other #1284
†Who's the Father of Jenny's Baby? #1302
The Boss and the Beauty #1342
His Ten-Year-Old Secret #1373

Her Dream Come True #1399
Adopted Dad #1417
His Wild Young Bride #1441
**The Nanny Proposal #1477
**The Doctor's Medicine
    Woman #1483
**Rachel and the M.D. #1489

*The Single Daddy Club
†Mother & Child
**Single Doctor Dads

babies
& BACHELORS USA

Donna Clayton
Fortune's Bride

Silhouette Books

Published by Silhouette Books
America's Publisher of Contemporary Romance

For Denise,
my bestest friend in the whole wide world.

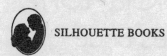

SILHOUETTE BOOKS

ISBN 0-373-82256-1

FORTUNE'S BRIDE

Visit Silhouette at www.eHarlequin.com

Printed in U.S.A.

Prologue

Lifting her face toward the sky, Laura Adams closed her eyes, dug her toes into the sun-heated sand and thought that nothing could spoil this perfect day.

"Mom!"

Brian's shout jerked her to attention.

Her six-year-old son ran toward her, frantically gesturing. "That little girl is lost."

Laura gazed down the beach where her son was pointing. Sure enough, a child walked on the damp sand near the water's edge, her long, blond hair tangled by the wind. She was small, a couple of years younger than Brian, by Laura's estimation.

Tourist season didn't officially begin until Memorial Day weekend, which was two weeks away. The beach was relatively bare of people, save for the few sun-worshipers enjoying the unusually warm spring day.

"Honey, there's a family right up there," Laura told her son. "I'm certain that little girl belongs with them and she's simply walked too far away, is all."

Brian's tiny frown grew as it planted itself firmly between his brows. "She's lost," he stated emphatically. "I've been watchin' her. She passed that family. Yes, sir-ree—" his little head bobbed up and down "—she's lost."

Laura tried not to grin at his insistent tone of voice. She was just about to suggest that they ask the girl if they could help her when Laura caught sight of a man running from the direction of the street. He called out to the little girl, but whatever he said was carried away by the salty breeze.

"There," Laura said. "There's her daddy. She's okay now." She patted her son's arm comfortingly.

Brian's eyes remained riveted to the girl. "That's not her daddy."

"Of course it is...."

Laura's voice died when a piercing scream erupted from the little girl. Her heart raced in her chest as she watched the man snatch up the child and hurry back in the direction of the street.

Could it be possible that the man wasn't the child's father—that he somehow meant her harm?

It was a fleeting thought, one that didn't even stay in her head long enough for her to take a quick breath. Such things simply didn't happen in a small family community like Dewey Beach.

The girl was obviously throwing a temper tantrum. Her father was undoubtedly angry that she'd gotten herself lost, that's why he was being so rough and so seemingly uncaring about his daughter's distress.

"Mommy."

Laura looked at her son. He hadn't called her that for months. He'd felt he was growing up and one way to prove it was to drop the childish parental reference. The look on Brian's face tore at Laura's heart. This scene was upsetting him as much as it was her.

She smoothed her palm down his forearm. "It's okay, honey."

"It's not." Brian's chin trembled and his eyes filled with tears. "That's not her daddy."

"What makes you say that, sweetheart?" Laura's question was full of tender patience, even though her insides quivered with her own doubt.

"I told you. She came from way up there." Once again he pointed up the beach.

Despite the sun's heat, a frightening chill crawled up Laura's spine. There could be a million reasons why the man hadn't come from the same direction as the little girl. A million reasons why an innocent scene like this could disturb an onlooker such as herself. But, if there was one chance in a million that this man was up to no good, one chance in a million that he was attempting to abduct this helpless child, could Laura sit and do nothing?

With the hot debate raging in her head, she pushed herself to a stand and absently brushed sand from the rear of her shorts.

If the stranger's intent *was* to carry away the girl, Laura's intervention could put her and Brian in danger.

What was she thinking? If that man meant to harm the child, she *had* to stop him. Still, her feet remained firmly planted on the sand as she battled her indecision.

The panicky cry that erupted from her son's throat was the motivating factor that finally pushed her into action.

Kneeling down, Laura settled Brian on the sand. "You sit right here," she said firmly. "I'll go see what's going on." She took off running, yelling over her shoulder, "Don't move, Brian. I'll be right back."

Excuse me, she mentally practiced, *can I point out the fact that your child is in hysterics? No, No. That's much too aggressive.*

Hello. I see your daughter's upset. I run a day care center and work with children every day, could I help you calm her down? Better, she thought.

The man was halfway to the street, so Laura sprinted across the sandy distance.

"Excuse me," she called.

The man ignored her.

"Hey!" she shouted. "Hey, you."

Laura was close enough now to hear the little girl screaming, "I want my Poppie," over and over. The child's frantic wiggles made it hard for the man to keep hold of her.

The man's flagrant disregard of her attempts to talk to him made Laura angry. It also made her certain that something devious was taking place here. A twinge of fear mingled with her anger.

"Hey, mister." She grabbed his arm and forced him to slow down.

He whirled on her. "Leave me alone, lady." He jerked his arm from her grasp and kept stomping forward.

"What's going on?" she demanded.

"I said, leave me alone!"

Fierce determination to get an answer to her question overrode her fear. Laura managed to get in front of him. He slowed down a little, but not much.

"Twenty-ish, five foot ten, frizzy red hair, lots of freckles," she spouted off his physical features above the child's wails. "I can give the police a pretty thorough description."

He cursed viciously and tried to shove her away, but the little girl's struggles made his effort all but nil.

Laura continued her litany, "Tattoo of snake on left biceps. 'Victor' tattooed on left forearm." She dragged her feet in the sand in an attempt to slow him further. "Is that your name? Hey, Victor, you're in deep trouble."

He came to a dead stop when she called him by name. He looked past her toward the street, and for a split second his uncertainty was obvious. The profanity that spewed from his mouth would normally have made Laura blush. He shoved the little girl at her and took off running.

Not expecting the weight of the child, Laura gasped as the sheer force of gravity toppled her, and she and the child fell to the sand.

The toddler howled with fright and confusion.

"It's okay, now," Laura soothed. "Everything's okay."

She sat up and held the little girl's trembling body.

"Mom! Mom! You did great, Mom." Brian plopped down next to Laura, kicking sand across her lap.

"I thought I told you not to move." Her tone was sharpened by the self-preserving fear that slowly returned her to her senses.

"But he's running away," Brian said. "See?"

Laura turned her head just in time to see "Victor" leap a small dune. He grabbed the hand of a thin, young woman whose long, blond hair whipped in a wide-arced curtain as the two of them ran out of sight.

The little girl's sobs had died to a quiet, hiccuping cry. Laura smoothed her hand over the tangled mass of baby-fine, flaxen curls.

"Come on, now," Laura crooned. "Everything's okay."

"The bad man's gone," Brian added confidently. "We'll help you find your mommy."

The child sniffed. "I don't have a mommy. I want Poppie."

"We'll find Poppie, I promise," Laura assured, handing her a tissue she'd pulled from her pocket. "Can you tell me your name?"

"Abbie," she said. "Abbie Mitchell."

"Well, Abbie, I'm Laura and this is Brian." Laura took each child by the hand and started up the beach in the direction Abbie had come from. "Is Poppie your grandfather?" The child nodded and Laura continued, "Well, first we'll find Poppie. And then we'll find a policeman. We wouldn't want that bad man trying to take off with someone else's child today, would we?"

Both Abbie and Brian shook their heads solemnly as the three of them trudged up the shoreline hand in hand.

That evening, Laura sat on her front porch and tried to relax. Brian was tucked in bed, and she slowly rocked in the wicker chair, her legs stretched out in front of her.

She could barely believe how her life had changed in one day. One afternoon, really. The mere thought brought giddy excitement to tickle her stomach, but she took a deep breath in an effort to quell it. Calm nerves and a clear mind would be essential if she were to utilize this unexpected windfall to her best advantage.

Laura let her thoughts retrace the events of the day—the events that had so changed her and her son's future. Little Abbie had squealed with joy as she had run into the open arms of her grandfather. Alfred Mitchell, his complexion gray with worry, had been overflowing with gratitude. The elderly man insisted on taking Laura and Brian to the nearest ice-cream parlor for a treat.

In the two hours they had spent together, Alfred had succeeded in drawing an abundance of information from her. He'd listened intently as she explained how she'd left her job as an elementary-school teacher when her son had been born in order that she could be home with him.

She shuddered now, remembering how Alfred had somehow pulled from her the dark memories of how her husband had slowly and painfully died from a cancer that defeated the best doctors available. Alfred had even evoked from her the lonely and frightening months after her husband's death, when she'd planned and then started her own in-home day-care business so that she could survive economically and still be with her young son.

A mosquito buzzed near her ear, and when the annoying insect landed on her forearm, she swatted idly at it. Now that she thought back on the afternoon, Laura realized that Abbie's Poppie had also succeeded in skillfully extracting from her all her hopes and dreams. He'd been so easy to talk to, so interested in her vision of her and her son's future. Alfred had seemed so impressed with her idea of expanding her in-home day care to a large, safe facility—a child-oriented environment where the emphasis was placed less on making money and more on creating a warm and loving atmosphere to which a parent could entrust his child's care.

She'd been left speechless when the old gentleman had finally revealed the fact that he wasn't just Alfred Mitchell, he was *the* Alfred Mitchell, president of Mitchell Corporation. The multi-million-dollar corporation was a heavyweight contender in the computer software industry.

When Alfred insisted on presenting her with a monetary reward for saving his granddaughter, Laura had objected, stating that she'd only acted as any decent human being would have. But with continued gentle persuasion and a touch of sheer obstinacy, Alfred was at last able to convince her that she should accept the reward.

Twenty-five thousand dollars.

A tingle of anticipation swept through her. She felt the need to pinch herself to make sure she wasn't dreaming. It was all so absolutely wonderful. Her plans were on the verge of fruition. Laura stood up and sighed. Nothing, absolutely nothing could spoil the happiness and fulfillment that Alfred Mitchell had given her today.

A pair of headlights rounded the bend, breaking into her reminiscence. The automobile pulled to the curb and stopped. She didn't know much about cars, but this one was black and sleek and elegant, something a person would expect to see on the glossy pages of *Car Design* or an equally exclusive magazine.

The man who emerged was as sleek and elegant as the shiny sports car. The dark, double-breasted suit on his taller-than-average frame had a European cut that emphasized his broad shoulders. His black hair was slicked straight back from his forehead and the moonlight glinted off its silky texture.

Laura instinctively knew he was unaware of her presence in the shadows of the porch. He approached the house, his movements like that of a predatory animal, smooth and precise, with no wasted motion. A powerful panther—that was the exact image he brought to mind. For one instant, the moonlight caught his face.

If good looks were a minute, then this man would be an hour and a half. Laura thought she spoke the words in her mind, but it was her murmuring voice that broke the night silence.

He stopped, his eyes piercing the cloaking darkness as he seemed to look straight at her. "Is someone there?" he asked.

Had she really said the words aloud?

She swallowed nervously, stepping from her dark

protection and into the silvery light of the full moon. She grasped the wooden railing.

His determined chin raised a fraction. "I'm looking for Laura Adams."

Laura tried to smile. "I'm Laura."

The man stared at her, long and hard. Then he announced, "I'm Dylan Mitchell. Abbie's father."

She relaxed a bit, the smile she'd tried to summon a moment before spread across her mouth. Abbie's father had come to thank her.

"It's nice to meet you, Mr. Mitchell." She descended the first step and offered her hand in welcome.

He didn't take it. In fact, he ignored it, expressing none of the expected friendly overtures of a first meeting. He looked at her hand, his lips compressed, his jaw tightened. And when he raised his gaze, his dark eyes narrowed to a glacial stare as he appraised her from head to foot and back again.

Laura was taken aback. Her hand slowly lowered of its own volition. She'd been praised by Alfred Mitchell, a police officer and a host of enthusiastic onlookers. Her own son had called her a hero for saving little Abbie from a would-be abductor. But the man standing before her had no intention of commending her, of that she was entirely certain.

"Just as I thought," he said quietly. "Gorgeous as all get out, with a body to match."

His condescending tone was meant to humiliate and it made Laura's face flush hot.

"I beg your pardon?"

"You can drop the act, Ms. Adams." The words were stone cold. "I'm on to you."

She opened her mouth to question the meaning of his blunt statement, but his continued hostile assault left her speechless.

"Women like you ought to be locked up," he said.

The harshness in his voice impelled Laura to take a backward step. She frowned and her natural reflex action brought her hand protectively to the base of her throat.

"How do you women live with yourselves?" he asked. "Taking advantage of people is a game to you, isn't it? You really should find a better way to make a living."

What was he talking about? How had she taken advantage of anyone by keeping a little girl safe from harm?

Again she opened her mouth to speak, but her body simply shut down. She couldn't get her lungs to pass air over her larynx. Words and questions jumbled in her head, but her lips had become useless.

"My father may be taken in by your big blue eyes and your charming smile," he snapped. "But, you can bet, I won't be suckered by a pretty face or pretty talk."

His disturbing accusation pierced the fog that numbed her brain. He obviously thought she'd done something inappropriate, that she'd somehow duped Alfred Mitchell. Finally, she found her voice.

"Mr. Mitchell, if you'll just stop a minute—"

"No, you stop," he said, cutting her off. "My father is a sick man. He doesn't have long to live. I will not stand by and let vultures like you take advantage of him."

"Alfred's dying?" The news hit her so hard that she barely heard the remainder of this man's angry words.

Alfred *had* looked ill, she remembered. She had attributed his gray coloring and unsteady demeanor to his being worried about his granddaughter. But, now, she was learning the truth.

And what had Dylan Mitchell just said? Something about her taking advantage of his father?

Her unseeing eyes grew wide and her fingers flew to cover her mouth. Had she taken advantage of a dying man?

"Ms. Adams—"

Dylan Mitchell's sharp tone tugged her back to the present.

"—it was extremely inappropriate for you to exploit my father's generous nature."

His observation was like a shovel full of hot guilt being piled onto her shoulders. Her chest became so tight with shame that she found it hard to draw in a breath.

"It would be best for everyone concerned," Dylan continued, "if you were to return the check. To me. Immediately."

The cold condemnation clearly written on Dylan

Mitchell's face made Laura feel felonious. Had she really taken advantage of a dying man? The question reverberated through her brain until it was impossible for her to think straight.

"The check, Ms. Adams. *Now.*"

"Of course." Her words were automatic and sounded far off to her own ears.

She didn't remember going inside the house to get the check or returning to the porch to hand it to the stern-faced man waiting there. But, blazed in her memory forever would be his taut little smile and his curt nod of victory as he plucked every hope and dream she'd ever had right from her fingertips.

Chapter One

Dear Ms. Adams:

This is to inform you that you have been named as a beneficiary of the recently deceased Alfred Mitchell. In accordance with the deceased's wishes, your presence is requested at the reading of a special letter, penned by Alfred Mitchell...

Welling tears blurred out the remaining words on the page and Laura felt an overwhelming sadness permeate her spirit. Alfred Mitchell, the kind gentleman whom she'd met just two short months ago, had died. He'd been one of the kindest people Laura had ever met. Alfred Mitchell had intended on giving her the world—until his son had intervened.

Now, now, Laura, she silently admonished herself.

Dylan Mitchell had only been trying to protect his father at a very vulnerable time in the old man's life.

But even though she knew Dylan had an excellent excuse for what he'd done, Laura couldn't help but feel insulted by how he'd made her out to be some kind of gold-digging opportunist.

She had felt horrible when she'd learned about Alfred's terminal illness, and guilt had very nearly smothered her when Dylan had pointed out that she'd taken advantage of his father's generosity. But, after she'd had time to think about it, she'd come to realize that Alfred Mitchell had *wanted* her to have that money. In fact, he'd felt so strongly about the matter that he'd actually talked her into taking it. She was sorry now that she'd ever let Dylan Mitchell make her feel guilty—so guilty that she'd relinquished to him the monetary gift that could have changed her future.

Laura had come to terms with the situation, though, thinking of the whole matter as water under the bridge. It was something she'd simply have to learn to live with.

Forcing herself to focus on the letter that had arrived in this morning's post, she couldn't stop the heartwarming smile that pulled at her mouth or the sentimental tears that threatened to spill as she remembered Alfred. As sick as he'd been, he hadn't forgotten her. The kind man had remembered her in his will.

He had tried to help her all those weeks ago, but

his efforts had been thwarted by his son. Now, he seemed to be reaching out to her again, bent on influencing her life.

Laura tipped up her chin. Well, if Alfred Mitchell wanted to bring some promise into her hardworking existence, who was she to deny him? If he wanted to leave her a legacy that might change her and her son's lives for the better, it would be stupid and downright rude to his memory for her to refuse.

With a fierce determination she decided that, regardless of whether her bequest was twenty-five thousand dollars or twenty-five cents, she'd accept the gift with a gracious and thankful heart. Dylan Mitchell be damned!

After pushing the button that would instruct the elevator to take her to the third floor, Laura watched the doors glide shut. The swift upward movement sent her already nervous stomach roiling. She pressed her flattened palm against her abdomen and prayed she wouldn't be sick. That's all she needed when she was about to meet Dylan Mitchell for the second time.

He was the reason behind her upset stomach, not the thought of inheriting some money, and certainly not this elevator ride. The very idea of coming face-to-face with the dominating Dylan was daunting enough to make her feel like a first-grader on the opening day of school.

The elevator doors slid open and her subconscious

kicked in, commanding her to exit. But the sight of Dylan Mitchell pacing like a caged animal at the other end of the hall riveted her feet to the floor.

His dark hair was swept back from his forehead and gleamed silkily in the artificial office light just as it had in the natural rays of the moon on the night she'd first met him. His dark suit hugged his broad shoulders and tapered to his trim waist. The pristine white shirt set off the teal paisley tie to perfection. His tailored attire magnified his sleek good looks. Yet, his coal-black eyes were lit with a predatory glimmer that once again reminded her of a panther. A hungry panther.

And suddenly those dark eyes were focused on her.

She'd expected to feel fear and intimidation when she saw Dylan Mitchell. And she did. But she also saw something unexpected in the coal-black depths of his gaze; she became clearly aware of the distress and grief emanating from him. The tightness around his mouth only proved to remind her that this man was mourning the death of his father. How could she have been so caught up in her own anxiety as to have forgotten that fact?

Laura berated herself for allowing her apprehension to paint a distorted picture of Dylan Mitchell. Sure, his behavior had been rapacious the night they had met—she even understood he'd thought he'd had good reason to take her money. But that didn't mean he would be like that now.

He took a step in her direction, and at the same time, she was surprised when the elevator doors began to close. Automatically, she stuck her hand in their pathway in order to set off the electric sensor that would reopen them.

The metal doors sprang back and Laura walked out into the plush-carpeted hallway. The look on Dylan Mitchell's face was weary, and she thought she read a touch of chagrin in his eyes, as though he was uncertain as to how she was going to react to him.

Well, he *should* feel uncertain. After the asinine way he'd treated her—

Now, now, she quickly admonished herself, *remember that the man had only been protecting his father.* Proper etiquette demanded that she at least declare the empathy she felt.

"I'm so sorry about your father," she told him. "He was one of the kindest men I ever met."

Usually, expressing condolences was awkward for Laura, but the words of solace slipped from her lips with ease because of the simple fact that they were true.

Dylan nodded his thanks. He looked past her a moment and she saw his jaw muscle tighten, then she watched his throat convulse in a swallow. It was obvious that Dylan was reining in his sorrowful emotions.

Something deep inside Laura called to her to reach out and touch him. She was flustered by the urge and fought it, uncertain as to why she felt it, how he would respond or if her support would even be accepted. With these confusing doubts rambling around inside her, she suddenly understood that grief was a universal emotion, one that caused great pain, one that was best expressed openly to someone who cared. And at this moment, she realized that she *was* someone who cared—if not about Dylan himself, at least about the fact that his father was no longer on this earth.

Laura placed her hand on his arm. Her touch drew his gaze, and she couldn't tell if it was his intense obsidian eyes or the feel of his tight, sinuous forearm that started her fingers tingling with a strong, uncanny awareness that made her uncomfortable. She was about to remove her hand when he lifted his and slid his warm, smooth palm over her fingers.

"Thanks," he said, his voice rusty with anguish.

For what? she wondered. Saying nice things about his father? Understanding his grief? Or caring enough to reach out and console him in his time of need?

Probably all of those things, she mused.

He cleared his throat. "I've been meaning to contact you."

"Oh?" She couldn't keep the astonishment from her voice.

He exhaled quickly in what Laura might have taken at any other time for a chuckle.

"After the way I acted," he commented, squeezing her fingers, "hearing from me is probably the last thing you ever would have expected."

Laura could feel her cheeks coloring as he voiced her very thought.

"It's okay," he assured. "I deserve it. My behavior that evening was inexcusable. I said things I shouldn't have and—"

"But you had good reason to do what you did," Laura said. "Your father was very sick. And he'd given a complete stranger a great deal of money."

What in heaven's name was wrong with her? She couldn't believe she was actually handing Dylan Mitchell an excuse for taking her reward. She understood his grief, but she didn't have to be an idiot about what he had done.

"Oh, I had reason, all right." Dylan's eyes hardened for a brief moment. "But the reason had nothing to do with my father's illness."

Taking her bottom lip between her teeth, she looked into his dark eyes. *What does he mean?* she wondered. Dylan had accused her that night of having taken advantage of his father. Now, the look of sheer bitterness that hardened Dylan's gaze intimated that something else could be blamed for his actions. But if it hadn't been his father's illness, what *had* spurred him to make the two-hour drive from the city of Wilmington to the small beach community of Dewey to retrieve her reward money? Curiosity fluttered inside her, but evidently Dylan wasn't going to be forthcoming with answers to her unasked questions. And besides, Dylan Mitchell's past, present or future were none of her business.

"Anyway," he said, "like I said, I've been meaning to call you. But since my father's death..."

He hesitated, and Laura could clearly tell the very words brought him pain.

After clearing his throat, he continued, "I've been trying to run the company on my own. It hasn't been easy. With Dad suddenly gone, it's as though the anchor has been torn from the ship during a terrible storm."

He paused a moment. "And then there's Abbie." He shook his head. "She was awfully close to her Poppie. She misses him terribly."

Dealing with death was one of life's hardest challenges. And because no one had all the answers as to why such things occurred, helping a child cope through the trauma was difficult, to say the least. Laura knew this firsthand as she'd gently guided her own son through his father's death just three short years ago.

But something nagged at the back of Laura's mind, yet before she could pull it to the forefront of her thoughts, he changed the subject.

"My father finally told me all about your heroism."

Dylan's proclamation turned her attention away from the troubling thought and she saw him give a sad little nod.

"He was bedridden by the time he came clean

with the true story." His tone grew pensive as he added, "It was as though he was giving me some kind of confession."

The blatant grief shadowing his features wrenched Laura's most tender emotions, and when he absently squeezed her hand, she became cognizant of the heated current humming in the nerve endings of her fingertips.

"You see," he said, "Dad lied to me about what happened that day at the beach." His gaze raised to the ceiling and he murmured, "Boy, did he lie."

Laura felt her brows knit together. "What do you mean?" she asked.

Dylan's breath escaped him in a sigh. "It's my fault, really. After my father discovered he was ill, he began taking Abbie to Dewey Beach every chance he got. They would drive down for the day, build a sand castle or two, have lunch and a nice long walk along the beach. They really enjoyed spending that time together."

Unconsciously—Laura was certain—he slipped his thumb into the valley between her own thumb and index finger where he slowly massaged a tiny circle.

"Dad had a bad spell," Dylan said, "a few days where he couldn't even get out of bed. I told him the trips to Dewey should stop. That the long drives, the stressful days were getting too much for him."

Laura tried to concentrate on Dylan's words, but more and more her attention was focusing on the tiny movement of the pad of his thumb against her tender skin. It was causing conflicting emotions within her; she wanted to pull away, yet at the same time she yearned to close her eyes and enjoy his touch. She *knew* he was unaware of his actions. And just as unaware of her *re*actions—thank heaven!

"Dad was so upset at the idea of my putting an end to his trips with Abbie," Dylan said. "When he was well enough to drive again, he insisted on taking her to the beach. I finally agreed, with a strict stipulation that if anything happened to upset him the trips would have to stop."

He inhaled deeply, and Laura forced herself to ignore the concentric circles of delicious heat caused by his unmindful caress. She needed to focus on the conversation.

"So when Abbie was nearly abducted, Dad felt that he had to lie to me." His tone held a weary quality. "He was so afraid that I'd refuse to let him take Abbie on any more outings." He leveled his gaze on her as he added, "And he was right, I would have."

Laura didn't know what to say. She understood Dylan's desire to protect his father's health and his daughter's safety, but at the same time she could sympathize with Alfred's need to get away with his granddaughter—especially since he *knew* his time with Abbie was limited.

A question fluttered at the edges of Laura's mind,

but it hadn't time to fully form before Dylan spoke again.

"Dad told me that Abbie got away from him. That you'd found her and saw that she got back to him safely." Dylan grinned rueful. "He tried to make light of having given you the money. I thought it was because he'd been embarrassed by having been taken in by you. Lord knows there are women out there ready, willing and able to cheat and deceive—" He stopped suddenly and took a deep inhalation before continuing. "The truth was that Dad didn't want me to know the real facts of the situation. That the check was a reward." Then Dylan grimaced. "Of course, my father's lie caused a whole chain reaction of misdeeds."

She felt the pressure of his firm fingers on her skin as he gently squeezed her hand again and her heart began to patter to a quick beat. Barely able to suppress a frown of confusion, she marveled at the magnitude of her physical awareness of this man.

"I flew to Dewey to do battle with you," he said. "I made light of your courageous behavior, and I succeeded in talking you out of your reward."

His blunt description of his actions—actions that had caused her weeks of heartache—brought back all the resentment she'd harbored against this man. Dylan Mitchell had stripped her of all hope of achieving her dream. Twenty-five thousand dollars was just a spit in the bucket to a man as wealthy as he, but he'd taken her money and driven off into the night with no thought of what he was doing to her.

And here she stood, feeling giddy and having heart palpitations from his touch. Her body was betraying her, damn it! She felt utterly disgusted with herself. Immediately, she pulled her hand from his grasp.

Dylan looked taken aback by her abrupt action, but at that moment the elevator bell rang its arrival, the doors slid open and a paunchy, balding gentleman stepped out to join them in the hallway.

"Good morning, Dylan. Sorry I'm late." The man reached out to shake Dylan's hand.

"How are you, Steve?" Dylan asked.

"Fine. Just fine," the man said, his tone gruffly businesslike.

"Laura, this is Steve Meekins, my father's attorney," Dylan introduced. "Steve, this is Laura Adams."

"Laura." The older man's face lit up like a bright light. "Alfred told me all about this brave lady."

Steve shook her hand so stoutly that Laura had to smile. "It's nice to meet you," she said.

"And it's great to meet you," the lawyer returned. "Alfred couldn't say enough good things about you. He must have told me the story of your saving Abbie at least a dozen times before he died. You were Alfred's champion, let me tell you."

Laura felt her face grow warm. "Please, Mr. Meekins, don't make more of it than—"

"Okay, okay," the lawyer said. "I didn't mean to

go on and on. Let's go into one of the conference rooms and we'll get down to business.''

Steve Meekins nodded to his secretary as he passed her desk. "Hold my calls, Jan," he told the woman.

She merely nodded efficiently and turned back to her computer.

Everything in the large room proclaimed affluence: the plush, steel-blue carpeting, the long, ornately carved walnut conference table, the elaborate molding at ceiling level, the gorgeous, heavy drapes that flanked the tall, narrow windows. The framed oil paintings were signed originals, the delicate beauty of which nearly took Laura's breath away.

Dylan directed her to a big leather chair, and after she'd perched on the very edge of the seat, he relaxed into the adjacent one as though he was right at home in such grand surroundings.

"Give me just a minute here to get myself together," Steve Meekins said.

As she watched him open his briefcase and extract a long manila envelope, Laura began to feel nervous and giddy. Was she really going to become twenty-five thousand dollars richer today? Was it possible that something so wonderful could happen? Or would Dylan try to deprive her of her money once again?

Her eyes narrowed. Let him try!

"Here we are," Steve said after clearing his

throat. He unfolded the typed pages and then perched a pair of reading glasses on his nose.

"Dear Dylan and Laura," the lawyer read. "If you are listening to this, then that means I must be dead. Don't feel sad for me, I'm in a much better place than you."

Laura gasped, horrified by the brusque opening, but a curt chuckle escaped from Dylan.

"That certainly sounds like my practical father, all right," Dylan commented.

"This message is mostly written to you, Laura," the lawyer continued. "Although I have a few choice words for my son."

Laura's stomach began to churn with anxiety.

Steve Meekins hesitated long enough for the message to penetrate, then he began to read again. "There aren't words to describe just how grateful I am that you saved my precious granddaughter. If you hadn't intervened that day on the beach, who knows what would have happened? Because the man was never apprehended, his intentions will never be known. Abbie could have been harmed. She could have been stolen, never to be seen again. Abbie could have been killed. Any of these things would have been tragedies that would have changed my life and my son's life completely."

The lawyer paused and nodded his agreement, and out of the corner of her eye, Laura saw Dylan press his lips together firmly. She couldn't help but wonder what he was thinking.

"Laura, I thank you," Steve proceeded to read from Alfred's letter. "I'm certain that Dylan thanks you also. And since he was so foolish as to take your reward money, he has given me an excellent opportunity to reward you again."

Dylan shifted in his seat and Laura forced herself not to look in his direction. This must be killing him.

The lawyer read on, "I intend to give you stock that will afford you ten-percent ownership of Mitchell Corporation."

"What!" Laura's tone was so loud, she immediately flushed with heated embarrassment. "Sorry," she muttered, and slid back into the seat, her mind reeling. Mitchell Corporation was a successful company. This gift of Alfred's had to be worth far more than her original twenty-five thousand dollars.

Wondering what Dylan's initial reaction to this revelation was, she cast a furtive glance his way. His jaw was clenched tight, but other than that his expression remained completely unreadable. He must be eating himself inside out over this turn of events.

Steve Meekins looked at her over the top of his glasses, and once she'd settled back into the leather chair, he continued, "This gift of stock will assure that Dylan will work with you on my idea. You see, after speaking with you, I decided that your dream of a large day-care center had a great deal of merit. I would like to have you go one step farther, though, and facilitate a child-care service for the employees of Mitchell Corporation."

Dylan leaned forward, listening intently.

The lawyer read on, "I'm certain my son will agree—after some discussion—that this is a great move for the company. Laura, I ask that you at least give my idea a try. If you feel you cannot work with Dylan then I will understand. I will stipulate, though, that if you decide to sell your portion of the company, you must give him first option of buying your stock. This will ensure the future of Mitchell Corporation and will give you the capital you will need to make your dream come true. But if you try my way first, you will have money, security *and* your dream."

Completely overwhelmed, Laura closed her eyes and rested her forehead in the palm of her hand.

"Are you all right, Ms. Adams?" the lawyer asked.

"Oh, yes," she said weakly, her throat convulsing in a dry swallow. "I just can't believe all this."

"I think it's pretty unbelievable myself," Dylan said. Almost as an afterthought, he curtly added, "I'm just finding out how foolish I was to talk you out of your original twenty-five thousand."

She didn't respond, refusing to be baited by his snide comment.

Steve Meekins caught their attention with a gentlemanly cough. "There's one more short paragraph."

Both Laura and Dylan turned to listen.

"In the short afternoon that I spent with you," the

lawyer read from the letter, "I found that you understood one of life's little secrets—a secret that took me many years to discover. I would request of you, Laura, to reveal this secret to my son."

Steve darted a glance at Dylan, then looked back at the paper in his hand. "I could spell it out, but I must admit that along with my sharp business sense, Dylan, you also inherited my thickheadedness. Oh, I'm certain that you're intelligent enough to understand the words, and you may even agree with them. It's just that I feel you wouldn't find it necessary to put them into practice. This lesson of life is best learned on one's own, before it's too late. And what better way to unlock the unknown than by spending time with someone who holds the key? Please understand that I only want the best for you, my son."

The lawyer paused and then stood. "Well, I'll leave you two—"

"That's it?" Dylan asked. "That's all there is?"

Steve Meekins nodded. "I'll step out and give you two some time alone. Don't rush."

"I can hardly believe this...." Laura felt so awestruck, the words tumbled from her lips before she could even think to stop them. Her conscience warred in her head; she wanted to giggle delightedly that Alfred had given her so much, but at the same time...

"I feel so bad," she said honestly. "This is your inheritance. I feel like I shouldn't have it."

His eyebrows rose the tiniest bit. "You want to refuse my father's bequest?"

The question froze her. She felt guilty, yes, but did she feel *that* guilty? She had Brian to think of. It didn't take her long to formulate an answer for him.

"I can't."

He simply stared at her with those dark, devouring eyes of his.

"I wish I could even apologize," she added with soft candor, "but I can't."

One of Dylan's shoulders lifted and then dropped. "I don't like the idea of losing ten percent of the company. But it seems this is what my father wanted." After a moment, he went on, "Dad was an excellent businessman. I trust his judgment implicitly. If he says your ideas about a corporate day-care center will be good for the company, then I believe it. Of course, it remains to be seen whether you can implement the ideas."

She felt a sudden flare of irritation at his doubt. But, again she refused to be pulled into an argument with this man. She'd simply show him that she was perfectly capable of handling this project.

A hazy happiness came upon her like a thick mist on a cool autumn morning. Her whole life was changing here, and it was going to take some getting used to.

"Ten percent..." Her tone held a large measure of amazement. "That's got to be worth more than my original reward."

Dylan's sharp laughter was unexpected and she bristled uncomfortably.

"Mitchell Corporation is a multi-million-dollar operation," he informed her. "Granted, most of that is in assets, but, yes, your portion is worth much more than your original reward."

"My," was all she could breathlessly say. When she reached up to swipe absentmindedly at a wayward strand of hair, she wasn't surprised to see her hand tremble. She looked at him with troubled eyes and asked, "Isn't there an inheritance tax in Delaware?"

"Don't worry," he said. "Mitchell Corporation has lawyers to handle that kind of thing. Someone will take care of all those details and make certain you understand what's happening."

The words afforded her a terrific sense of relief.

Then Dylan leaned closer to her. "Since Dad made certain we'd be working together, why don't you tell me what the two of you had in mind."

"But we didn't," she rushed to say. "Have anything specific in mind, I mean. I simply confided in Alfred that I wanted to open a large day-care center for children."

It looked as though Dylan's mind was churning, hard and fast. "A corporate day-care facility right on the property *is* a good idea. Do you think you could handle a center that large?"

"I know I can," she responded.

"Then let's talk business."

Over the next half hour, they discussed many aspects of the idea, from the number of children the day care would need to support, to the necessity of Laura and her son moving to the city of Wilmington.

"We can get you hooked up with a reputable real-estate agent," Dylan recommended. "In the meantime, you can stay in the guest cottage on the estate. It's small, but it has every modern convenience you could need."

"That sounds good, if you're sure my son and I won't be intruding." Laura's stomach hadn't stopped jumping since she'd entered the conference room. There was one big problem that she really wanted to address, and she knew there was no other way to go about it than to simply blurt it out. "I have something I need to say."

"Certainly," Dylan said.

She nibbled on her lower lip, unsure of how to phrase what she wanted to say. Then, she inhaled deeply and began, "I know nothing about running a large corporation." She nibbled her lip again and searched his gaze before continuing, "I'm going to have enough on my plate to get the day care off the ground and running." Again, she hesitated. "I'd like to know if you would...if you don't mind, I mean...could I just..." She exhaled in frustration and blurted out, "I want to focus my attention on the day care...I'd rather not mess with...with any corporate doings."

He was quiet for a moment, then he said, "I don't

have a problem with that. But in your own best interests, I think you should understand what's going on. We could meet periodically and I'll explain any changes that I've made and why. And at the same meeting, you can keep me abreast of what's happening with the new facility.''

It was as though a great burden had been lifted from her shoulders. She smiled and stuck out her hand.

''It's a deal,'' she said.

When his strong, elegant hand gripped hers, she became instantly aware of the heat that penetrated her skin. It seemed as if the two of them were charged with a low-voltage current that pulsed and snapped between them.

That's ridiculous, she told herself. It was just the excitement she felt concerning this dramatic change in her life. Nevertheless, when she pulled her hand from his, it was with reluctance.

''So,'' he said, resting one elbow on the tabletop, ''are you going to reveal this secret that Dad spoke of?''

She sighed. ''I've been wondering about that....'' She looked away, then turned to gaze directly into his eyes. ''You see, I have no idea what he was talking about.''

His brow wrinkled with a mixture of confusion and intrigue. ''But he said you knew.''

Laura shrugged and shook her head in bewilderment.

"Well, when the two of you were together, what did he have to say? What did you talk about?" he asked.

"That's what's so funny," she said. "He didn't say much. He kept the conversation on me—my life, my hopes, my dreams." Again she shook her head, this time in frustration. "He seemed to pull my life story from me and I didn't even know it was happening."

"So, he never mentioned this secret to you?"

She felt awful knowing that she wasn't helping him figure out the mystery his father had left, but she had to answer honestly. "No," she said.

Dylan leaned back in the chair and tapped his chin with his index finger.

"Well," he said, "it looks as though we'll have to figure this thing out together."

Chapter Two

"Here comes Abbie again." Brian had a sigh in his voice as he turned from the window.

"Does that bother you?" Laura asked as she neatly flipped the pancake in the skillet.

Since Laura and Brian had moved to Wilmington a week ago, little Abbie spent a majority of her time at the guest cottage. The toddler had taken to Brian like sticky to a lollipop. The elderly Mrs. Nichols, Abbie's live-in sitter, was happy for any reprieve she could get since the woman's duties also included housekeeping and cooking for Dylan and his daughter.

"No," Brian said, "I don't mind. It's just that she runs me ragged."

The exhausted tone in her son's voice caught her off guard and Laura stifled a chuckle. But despite his minor, verbal grievances, she felt her son enjoyed playing his role as the "big brother."

"She spends so much time here," Brian observed. "It's almost like we're her family."

Turning back to the stove, Laura made a point not to comment as she scooped the pancake from the pan and placed it on the stack with the others. Brian *was* right. Abbie had latched onto them tightly.

Dylan left for work at first light and didn't return until after dinner. Over the past week, Laura had had two meetings with him concerning the day-care facility, and those had been squeezed into his busy schedule. Laura had come to the inevitable conclusion that Dylan was a workaholic.

And she had come to understand that Dylan's work habits were the crux of the secret Alfred Mitchell had spoke of in his letter. Because Dylan spent so much time at Mitchell Corporation, he had little to no time to spend with his daughter. That was in direct opposition to Laura's parenting philosophy. Not that she didn't believe in hard work by any means; she simply felt that family should come first.

Alfred had known that she'd quit her job as a schoolteacher, that she'd started an in-home day-care center just so she could be with Brian.

Yes, Laura was certain that Alfred wanted her somehow to make Dylan realize that the important thing in life was knowing and raising his daughter. The question was *how*.

How could she convey to Dylan the importance of

being a good parent without insulting or offending him? Should she say nothing and simply show him, through her own parenting practices, Alfred's "secret"? Laura heaved a sigh as she put down the spatula.

"Can I eat?"

Laura turned to see Abbie gazing up at her and realized she'd been so focused on her thoughts she hadn't heard the little blond-headed beauty come inside.

Smiling down at the child, Laura couldn't help but think once again how those big, innocent blue eyes combined with all those flaxen curls made for a most angelic image.

"Didn't Mrs. Nichols fix breakfast for you?" Laura asked.

Abbie wrinkled her nose. "Yeah, but Nana cooked oatmeal. I like pancakes better."

"Come and sit down," Brian said hurriedly, as though Laura might not allow Abbie to eat with them.

Seeing her son's protective nature toward Abbie gave her heart a warm tug.

"Yes," she told Abbie, "sit down and I'll get you a plate."

Laura stacked two pancakes on Abbie's plate and Brian helped her pour the syrup.

"Are you sick?" Abbie asked Laura before stuffing a wedge of pancake into her mouth.

The question surprised Laura and she looked at

Abbie. A dribble of syrup ran down the child's chin. Handing her a napkin, Laura said, "Take smaller bites, and here, wipe your mouth. I feel fine. Why do you ask?"

Abbie took another bite, chewed a few times, then filled her cheeks so she could say, "You didn't go to work."

"It's Saturday, Abbie," Brian pointed out. "Mom doesn't work on Saturdays."

Abbie silently digested this, a frown nestled between her long-lashed eyes. She swallowed and then looked up at Brian.

"My daddy works every day."

The touch of confusion that tinted Abbie's words pulled at Laura's tender emotions. Sympathy for this child welled up inside her like a tidal wave. Laura didn't know what to say. Dylan Mitchell was letting the best years of Abbie's life slip like sand through his fingers. But how could you tell a little girl that her father was making a grievous mistake?

"Your daddy must be pretty important," Brian said.

Leave it to her six-year-old to save the day, Laura mused, smiling.

"He is," Abbie agreed. She looked from Brian to Laura, and back to Brian. After a moment, she wistfully added, "But it'd be nice if he was havin' pancakes with me."

Laura's smile faded. This little girl, with her innocent observations, was going to wrench from

Laura every ounce of empathy she possessed. Wanting to hide her reaction from Abbie, she nonchalantly covered her mouth with her hand and rested her chin in her palm.

At that instant, she was struck with an idea.

"How about if we have lunch with your dad?" She asked the question before she'd thought through the notion completely.

"You mean go to Daddy's work?" Abbie asked, her face beaming.

A thousand thoughts ran riot in Laura's head. She didn't even know if Dylan was at Mitchell Corporation. What if she was setting Abbie up for a disappointment?

"Yes," she answered emphatically, disregarding her doubts. "We'll go to your daddy's office. In fact, we'll pack a lunch and take him to the nearest park."

Abbie squealed with delight.

"Can I come?"

Laura looked over at Brian's questioning countenance.

"Of course you can come," she told him. "Now, finish up your breakfast. We have some chores to do before we can go."

"I can dust," Abbie pronounced. "Nana lets me help all the time."

"Good," Laura said. "I'd love to have your help."

"So would I." Brian's eyes twinkled with mischief.

Laura waggled her finger at him. "Don't think you're going to get Abbie to pick up your room," she said. "That's your job."

"Awww, Mom."

The morning passed swiftly, and before Laura even had time for a break, she found herself packing up sandwiches, fruit and boxes of juice. She didn't have a picnic basket, so she used the next best thing: one of the small, leftover moving boxes.

She called to let Mrs. Nichols know that she was taking Abbie to Mitchell Corporation. The older woman clicked her tongue in disapproval, murmuring something to the effect of, "Dylan's a busy man." But Laura didn't let that stop her. She was doing this for Dylan's own good. Besides, this was something Alfred wanted her to do. Why then, as she pulled into the parking lot of Mitchell Corporation, did she feel this tremendous anxiety nibbling like a mouse at her nerves?

Yet, despite the apprehension, she couldn't deny the powerful anticipation that caused her heart to flutter when she thought of seeing Dylan. Both times she'd met with him at his office this week had been hectic and rushed, but the undercurrent of awareness had been fully charged. It wasn't that he'd said or done anything to make her feel he was attracted to her. However, there had been unspoken messages in his obsidian gaze, in the stance of his tall, solid body, in the touch of his fingers on her hand when he sought her attention. These silent communications revealed a great deal to her. Or at least she thought they did.

But what if she was mistaken? The question made a quiver of doubt shimmy across her skin. Her physical reaction to Dylan had been clear and strong from the very beginning. She'd felt as though they shared something...some zesty chemical bond, some spicy kind of blend. Like salt and pepper.

Laura nearly laughed at her choice of analogy as she showed her identification badge to the security guard at the front door and then guided the children down the long hallway toward Dylan's office.

Doubt made her hesitant, though. She didn't want to embarrass herself by fabricating an interest on his part where none existed, so she'd adopted a "wait and see" attitude. And that attitude was what caused this overwhelming tingling of anticipation about seeing him again.

"Where is everybody?" Abbie asked.

The offices were empty, the halls almost eerily quiet. Looking down at Abbie's face, Laura sighed. She didn't want to make the child feel badly about having a father who worked incessantly, yet she had to admit, "Not too many people work on the weekend."

"Oh," was all Abbie said.

Finally, Brian pointed to the name plate on the door. "Look," he said, "there's Dylan's office."

Although the large reception area was brightly lit,

the room looked deserted and the secretary's desk was clear. Dylan's door was closed.

"Nobody's here," Abbie remarked, disappointment flattening her tone.

"We should knock just to make sure," Laura said. She tapped on the door and then opened it to peek inside. Her hopes of getting Abbie and her father together for lunch were dashed at the sight of the empty office.

She turned to Dylan's daughter.

"I'm sorry, Abbie. Your dad isn't—"

Just then Dylan came from what looked to be a file room. At the sight of them, his face was lit with a bright smile.

"Hi, guys," he said. "What's going on?"

"Daddy!"

Abbie ran and jumped into her father's arms. Laura smiled when Dylan bent to pick up his daughter and swooped her into the air.

"Hey, Pumpkin." He planted a kiss on her cheek.

This tender scene warmed Laura's heart, but the sight of Dylan with his shirt-sleeves rolled up to reveal corded, muscular forearms and long, strong hands stirred darker, more intense emotions in her. Absently, she ran her fingers through her wispy bangs and ran her tongue across her lips.

After planting his daughter on his hip, Dylan directed his gaze at Brian.

"Hey, buddy," he said. "How are you?"

"Okay." Brian shrugged.

Then Dylan's coal-colored eyes were on her and Laura felt her whole body grow warm. He looked so handsome, standing there with his top shirt button undone, his loosened tie askew.

Evidently sensing her attention on his attire, he reached up with his free hand to straightened his tie.

"I wasn't expecting you," he said.

"Please," she said, "it's okay. We just came for a visit."

"I'm glad."

His simple statement started her insides jittering. Laura managed a shaky smile in response and wished he had smiled at her.

"We brought lunch," Abbie announced.

"You did?" Dylan tickled his daughter's tummy and she giggled.

"Yeah," the child continued. "And we're going to the park. All of us. One, two, free—" she pointed to each of them as she counted, ending with a plump index finger on her own chest "—five."

"Four," Brian automatically corrected.

The look on Dylan's face showed his pleasant surprise. "Why, Abbie, I didn't know you could count."

"Brian's teachin' me."

"That's wonderful," Dylan said, looking at Brian. He tickled Abbie again. "I'm so happy you're learning your numbers." He kissed her cheek again and put her down. "But I really can't go to lunch today. I'm busy working."

Laura tensed.

"But it's *Saturday*," Abbie lamented.

Pressing her lips together, Laura felt bad. She'd known Abbie would put two and two together. It was only natural for the child to wonder why her daddy worked when the rest of the office took the weekends off.

Dylan crouched down to Abbie's level. "I know it is, Pumpkin. But Saturday is the only time I can spend going over the tax accountant's notes. I'm too busy during the week with the other researchers developing new software programs, and then there's the sales figures to go over and advertising brochures to update...." He lifted one shoulder. "And about a million other things."

He touched the tip of his finger to his daughter's nose. "You understand, don't you?" Then he stood and gazed apologetically at Laura.

Abbie looked brokenhearted and Laura's mind whirled with possible solutions.

Finally she blurted, "Well, you have to eat, don't you?"

Dylan just looked at her.

"We can eat here," she said. "Right in your office. And we won't take long, will we, kids?"

"Can we, Daddy?" The look on Abbie's face and the tone of her voice was pleading.

Dylan didn't hesitate. "Of course we can," he said.

Laura caught his gaze in hers. "I'll just run out to the car for the sandwiches—"

"Let's all go," Dylan said.

Abbie laughed with delight and took off down the hallway.

"I'll get her," Brian offered and ran after her.

Laura watched him go and then turned to Dylan. "I think my son just wanted a reason to run down the hall."

"It's okay. They can't hurt anything."

They fell into step together, and his solid warmth beside her felt...right somehow. It was silly, she knew, but she couldn't help what she was feeling.

"I'm sorry if we're bothering you," Laura said. She wasn't sorry in the least, but she felt this was the polite thing to say.

"Not at all," he assured her. "I'm happy to see you." As an afterthought, he added, "And the kids."

Those three little words he'd thrown in at the end made her certain that he'd meant "you" in the singular—as in *her*. A delicious chill went up her spine and her mouth spread in a exhilarated smile. She couldn't help it, and could do nothing to stop it.

"What is it?" he asked.

Self-consciously, she pressed her fingertips to her lips and dipped her head from his view.

"Nothing," she blatantly lied.

When she looked at him again, there was a tiny, quizzical frown on his brow. She was afraid he'd press her, but by then they had reached the children, who waited at the heavy glass doors.

"Going home so early, Mr. Mitchell?" the burly security guard asked.

"Oh, no, Sam. We're going to have lunch, is all."

The man nodded. "You have two cute kids there," the guard continued. "I don't think I ever saw your kids before."

Dylan picked up Abbie and she squealed with delight. "Abbie here is my little pumpkin," he explained. "Brian belongs to Laura. Laura Adams, meet Sam Bristow. Sam's my weekend Security."

Laura shook hands with the man.

"Nice to meet you, Ms. Adams. Mr. Mitchell and I have spent lots of weekends together."

No offense, Sam, Laura thought, *but I hope to change that.*

They retrieved the boxed lunch from the car and Dylan carried it back to his office. Laura set the sandwiches on paper plates and poked small, plastic straws into the boxes of juice while Dylan handed out napkins and the children settled themselves on the carpeted floor.

"An inside picnic!" Abbie's eyes were bright with excitement.

Brian helped Laura pass out the plates.

"Mmm," Dylan commented. "I haven't eaten peanut-butter-and-jelly in ages."

"My favorite," Abbie said, chomping a big bite.

Laura tucked her feet beneath her, and after taking

a sip of juice, she said, "We were going to go to Rockford Park. It's too bad you can't join us."

Dylan swallowed and wiped his mouth with a napkin. "I've lots of work to do. Quarterly taxes are due soon."

Abbie dusted crumbs from her fingers and stood up. "Daddy, I know a song. Wanna hear it?"

He reached up and gently swiped the peanut butter from her chin. "I'd love to hear it."

"I'm a little teapot, short and stout," she sang. "Here is my handle—" she plunked one fist on her hip "—here is my spout." The other hand stuck out straight to form a spout. "When I get all steamed up, then I shout. Just tip me over—" Abbie bent over so her "spout" pointed toward the floor "—and pour me out."

Dylan applauded his daughter. "That was wonderful!" He looked at Brian. "Did you teach her that song?"

"Naw," Brian said.

"Nana did," Abbie told her father.

"Well, it was very well done."

Abbie beamed with pride.

"Dylan, did you know that Abbie can sing the alphabet?" Laura asked.

Without waiting to be prompted further, Abbie launched into her own, slightly off-key version of the "ABC Song."

Laura, Brian and Dylan clapped after the performance.

Watching Dylan's gaze turn tender when he looked at Abbie, Laura felt certain that this man loved his daughter. He could be a wonderful father, a terrific father, if only he'd spend more time doing just that—being a father.

All through lunch, Laura made a point of verbally recognizing Abbie's many childhood accomplishments, which she'd discovered over the past week. She tried to be nonchalant, but she really wanted to determine how well Dylan knew his daughter. From what she was learning, he didn't know Abbie very well.

As Laura collected the plates and napkins, she commented, "Did you know that Abbie helps Mrs. Nichols with the household chores?"

Abbie nodded her head. "Nana lets me dust."

"And Abbie helped Brian pick up his room this morning, even though it was supposed to be his job," Laura added. "Isn't that right, Brian?"

A loud slurping sound reverberated from Brian's empty juice container as he nodded his head affirmatively. "That's right," he proclaimed, obviously not the least bit guilty that Abbie had done his work.

Dylan gave one of Abbie's blond curls a gentle, affectionate tug. "My little girl is really growing up."

"She sure is," Laura agreed pointedly.

When Dylan cast a curious glance her way, Laura realized that she'd placed too much emphasis on those last three words. Maybe she'd even gone a little overboard in her effort to get Dylan to notice his daughter.

"Abbie," Dylan said, "why don't you go out to my secretary's office and find the cup of pencils on her desk. You can use some of the plain paper that's next to the big copy machine, and you and Brian can draw some pictures."

Evidently loving the idea, the four-year-old hurried out the door.

"Would you help Abbie, Brian?" he asked.

"Sure."

Once Brian had left the room, Dylan turned to Laura.

"Okay," he said, "what's this all about?"

A rush of warmth spread across her cheeks. She could play innocent, but would that really be fair to Dylan? The honest truth might be hard for him to take. However, the plain fact of the matter would be better than playing games.

She searched his gaze a moment before she said, "You don't seem to know your daughter very well."

He didn't comment right away. He simply sat there, looking at her.

Finally, he said, "I'm not sure what you're getting at. I love Abbie very much."

"Dylan, I'm not accusing you of not loving Abbie," she hurried to assure him. Although a sudden case of nerves made her hesitate, she refused to back down now. "I *am* accusing you of not giving her what she needs."

"What? How can you say that? You don't know me. And you don't know my daughter."

Anger bunched in his shoulders under the cotton fabric of his dress shirt and she felt the urge to lean back away from him. Once again, she was reminded of a wild, predatory jungle animal. Her heart pounded, and she wondered if she would have been better off keeping her opinions to herself.

"I give my daughter a warm, solid house to live in. She has good, nourishing food, and Mrs. Nichols takes good care of her."

His jaw tensed, and Laura saw something else glimmering in his dark eyes besides the anger—she saw hurt. She felt terrible knowing she'd injured his feelings, and his pride. That was the one thing she hadn't wanted to do.

"Abbie has everything a child could need," Dylan went on. "Or want."

"Please." She raised her hands in surrender. "I never meant to…I'm really sorry that I…" Her voice trailed off. She took a deep breath to calm her jangling nerves. Then she quietly tried again. "Dylan, I'm only trying to obey Alfred's wishes."

Dylan frowned, and Laura felt the oddest urge to reach up and smooth away the tiny crease between his dark brows.

"What does my father have to do with this?" he asked.

There was so much to explain, Laura didn't know

where to begin. So she simply said, "Remember the secret he mentioned in his letter to us?"

Dylan rested his elbow on his bent knee and slowly nodded.

"Well…" Laura shrugged one shoulder a fraction. "I figured out what he was talking about."

He straightened his spine defensively. "Are you telling me that Dad thought I was a lousy parent?"

"No!" The tiny word rushed from her lips. "I'm saying nothing of the kind." She reached up and tucked a strand of hair behind her ear. "Dylan, this week I went over and over the conversation I had with your father. And then I started noticing little things about you and Abbie, like your leaving for work so early and coming home so late, and Abbie spending so much time either by herself or at the guest cottage with me and Brian. I simply put everything together—"

"And came up with the secret," he supplied.

"Um-hmm," she said.

He looked away as though steeling himself for the next part of their conversation. Then he directed that intense, charcoal gaze of his at her.

"I need you to tell me about this…secret."

Laura felt she needed to ease into the explanation, so she started off telling him about the talk she'd had with Alfred, how she'd been a teacher for several years, how she'd quit her job when she'd given birth to Brian, how she'd helped her son through his fa-

ther's death and then opened an in-home day-care
center so she could raise him.

She hesitated only long enough to take a breath
when he interrupted.

"Are you telling me I can only be a good parent
if I quit my job?"

His question dripped with sarcasm, and Laura felt
a spark of irritation. Why did he refuse to understand
that she was only trying to help him? But relenting
to her anger would only make the situation worse.

"No," she calmly said, "I'm not saying you
should quit your job. And I'm not going to fight with
you, so please stop goading me."

As if in slow motion, Laura watched his hand
move up to rub across his jaw. He had such strong
hands, she noticed.

"You're right," he said. "I shouldn't be angry
with you. It's just that this secret thing seems to be
directed at me…at my inadequacies. And it has me
feeling…"

"Defensive?"

He chuckled. "Exactly."

She gave him a reassuring smile. "Your father
never implied that you were inadequate in any way.
And Abbie loves you so much. She talks about you
incessantly."

His eyes found hers. "She does?"

Laura nodded. "I think all Alfred wanted was for
you to get to know Abbie. Strengthen your relation-

ship. Spend some time with her. Enjoy her. Like he did.''

''My father worked longer hours than I ever have.'' That stiff, defensive stance was back in his shoulders again. ''From my earliest memories, Dad was never around. He wasn't there for my mother. And he wasn't there for me.'' He sighed. ''Now, don't get me wrong. I loved my dad. He did the best he could. Gave me everything I could want. But it wasn't until he got sick that he started taking time off....'' His voice faltered and his eyes took on a faraway look, as though he'd been hit with a startling revelation. Finally, he directed his gaze at her. ''And he started spending it with Abbie.''

Laura's nod was nearly imperceptible. It was evident to her that Dylan finally understood.

''That's what Alfred meant,'' she murmured softly, ''when he said he didn't find out what was important in life until it was too late.'' She touched Dylan's knee. ''Your dad wanted you to have lots and lots of time with Abbie. Not just a few short months.''

He reached down and covered her fingers with his smooth, warm palm.

''Do you really think that's what he was trying to tell me?''

Laura knew he wasn't looking for an answer to his question. This was simply his reaction to a huge discovery. His reaching out to her was instinctive, one person's need of support from another in a time of eye-opening disclosure.

"Laura."

His whispering her name set the tiny hairs on the back of her neck standing on end. It sounded so melodic, so beautiful coming from his lips.

"I can't believe it," he continued, his tone husky with emotion. "I was doing to Abbie the very thing my father had done to me. I was being the same kind of parent Dad had been."

He cleared his throat and gazed off into the far corner of the room. She could see by the look on his face just how upset he was.

"My dad worked so hard," he said. "All the time. My mom was the one who raised me, really. I played lots of sports when I was young. Football, soccer, baseball. It was always my mother who came to watch the games. My mom was the one who took me to school functions. To church on Sundays."

His words were a monotone litany of memories. Laura did the only decent thing she could—she listened.

Finally, he looked at her for the first time in many minutes and said, "I did love my father. And I harbor no bitterness toward him. We had a wonderful relationship at the end." He shook his head. "But when I was growing up, I missed him like hell." His Adam's apple convulsed with a difficult swallow. "I just can't believe I was doing that to Abbie."

Laura squeezed his fingers. "But you can change all that. You can change it today."

"I will," he vowed. "I'll change." He lifted her hand and enveloped it in both of his. His gaze settled on her face for several long moments before he asked, "Will you help me?"

Laura's eyes widened. His question caught her completely off guard and made her emotions run riot. He was asking for her help. Why should that make her feel such happiness...such apprehension...such amazement...such confusion?

Despite the turmoil roiling inside her, she smiled softly and said, "Of course I will."

Chapter Three

"Take me out to the ball game. Take me out with the crowd."

Brian's high-pitched voice quavered off key as he soloed the all-time-favorite sports tune. Laura gazed at him and didn't even try to fight the warm smile that curled the corners of her mouth.

"Buy me some peanuts and Cracker Jack..."

Dylan's deep, rich baritone turned the song into a duet and Laura's smile widened to an out-and-out grin. She watched him pay the cashier, slip his wallet into his back pocket and take the tickets from the young woman in the glass booth.

Laura took Abbie by the hand and the four of them headed for the stadium steps. All the while Dylan and Brian continued to sing.

Abbie's eyes grew large with wonder as she

passed through the metal turnstile and out onto the large concrete area above the bleachers that afforded them an unobstructed view of the grassy playing field.

"Where do we sit?" Brian asked Dylan.

"Let's see." Dylan studied the ticket stubs for the exact seating section. "We should be directly behind home plate. Here we are."

The four of them had descended the bleacher steps about halfway when Abbie stopped dead.

"What's that?" she asked.

The sudden fear in the child's voice made Laura frown, and she looked out toward third base where Abbie's attention was riveted. But the creases in her forehead smoothed the instant she saw the huge, blue creature dancing and cavorting to entertain the pre-game crowd.

"That's the mascot of the Blue Rocks baseball team," Laura explained. "You don't need to be afraid."

But it was obvious Abbie didn't believe her, because the child inched her way over to her father and tugged lightly on his trousers. He bent over and pulled her up into a secure, two-armed embrace. Laura felt a warm tug on her emotions as she watched Dylan instinctively give his daughter the refuge she so desperately sought.

"Don't let it get me," Abbie pleaded softly.

"It's okay, honey."

Dylan's gentle, reassuring tone squeezed at

Laura's heart like a vice. But it wasn't a hurtful pain by any means; it was a nice, heated feeling that made her skin prickle with pleasure.

"There's a person inside that suit," he explained.

"There is?"

Laura could tell from Abbie's inflection that she didn't entirely believe what her dad was telling her.

"Sure there is," Dylan asserted. "There isn't a real animal that has blue fur."

"That's right, Abbie," Brian said. "There are tropical birds that are blue, but they have feathers, not fur."

Abbie looked from Brian to her dad to the big, lumbering creature that turned a somersault on the third baseline. As she settled herself closer against her father's chest, her mouth quirked into a nervous smile that told everyone she still wasn't entirely convinced of her safety.

"It's okay," Dylan told her as he smoothed the hair back from her face. "You just stick with me."

"Thanks, Dad." Abbie pressed her lips against his cheek.

Laura looked away, certain the heartwarming scene would make her throat close with emotion. Dylan might be a workaholic who spent very little time with his daughter, but there was no doubt that he loved the child dearly. Now that Laura had pointed out the fact that he needed to nurture and enrich his relationship with his daughter, maybe all the pieces would fall into place for Dylan and Abbie. Laura sincerely hoped so.

There was something about Dylan, Laura realized, that made her wish for his happiness. Maybe it was because his father had so recently passed away and her sympathy was running high—maybe it was because her own close and loving bond with Brian was so wonderful that she wanted Dylan to share the same with his daughter—maybe it was because...

The four of them found their seats and Laura let her mind wander as she tried to figure out exactly why she longed so deeply for Dylan's peace and contentment. She cast a sidelong glance at his profile. What was it about him, she wondered. Why did she feel this tremendous tug on her feelings where he and Abbie were concerned? Why did it seem as though she had this huge emotional investment in them?

She worried her bottom lip between her teeth, thinking back to a few days ago when Dylan had asked for her help in becoming a better parent—a better father. He'd opened himself up to her. He'd made himself so very...vulnerable. And she'd found that so very...appealing. Up to that point, he'd presented himself as self-assured, aggressive, poised; someone cool under pressure, and, yes, even wary. But in that one unguarded moment when he'd exposed his innermost feelings, when he questioned himself as a father, she'd empathized with him, she'd felt closer to him than she'd ever thought possible.

In fact, she could almost say that she'd felt something close to—

The crowd applauded as the baseball players took the field to warm up, shaking Laura from her musings. Dylan, Abbie and Brian shouted and laughed enthusiastically, and Laura was thankful for the diversion from the intimate track her thoughts had been veering toward.

Two of the Wilmington Blue Rocks players were at the base of the bleachers handing out something to the children.

"Baseball cards! Can I go down, Mom?" There was eager excitement in Brian's voice. "Can I?"

"It's 'may I,'" Laura corrected, "and, yes, you may."

"Do you have a piece of paper and a pencil?" he asked. "Maybe they'll give me an autograph."

Laura rummaged in her purse for a scrap of paper. "All I can find is a pen," she said, handing the items over to her son.

"I want to go, too!" Abbie piped up.

"It's okay," Brian told his mother. "I'll hold Abbie's hand."

Laura looked at Dylan. He darted a glance down the short, two-aisle space between where they were sitting and where the players were handing out the cards. He smiled and nodded at Brian.

"Go ahead," Dylan said. "Just be careful on the steps."

"We will," Brian promised.

Laura and Dylan watched as their children descended the concrete steps and waited patiently to meet the real live ball players.

After a moment of silence, Dylan murmured, "I can't believe Abbie's never been to a baseball game."

She watched his throat convulse in a tight swallow. His jaw tensed, and her eyes were drawn to the tiny, intense contraction of the muscle. She was startled by the feeling that exploded in her stomach—something akin to seismic activity down deep where her diaphragm pressed against her rib cage. Lord, but this man was attractive!

She inhaled deeply to clear her thoughts. This wasn't the time to become infatuated with Dylan Mitchell. Not when he was feeling so badly about himself as a parent. She should be comforting him, not admiring the way his jaw tightened so sexily. It took some doing, but she forcefully pushed the idea from her mind.

His contemplative gaze raised to hers. "I can't help but wonder about all the other things she's missed out on."

There was a sad pitch to his voice, a vulnerable note that ripped Laura's emotions like dry, brittle paper. Instinct alone made her reach out to him.

His hand was lean and strong beneath hers. The dark, springy hairs brushed lightly against the sensitive skin between her fingers. Blood pulsed through his veins; she could actually feel the beat under her fingertips.

Suddenly she was overwhelmed by a strange mixture of emotions; she wanted to comfort and protect, yet she couldn't deny the dark and heated sensuality that permeated every fiber of her being. She felt her face grow warm, even on this hot August evening. No, she couldn't deny what she felt, but she didn't have to reveal it, either.

The small smile that tilted her lips, she knew, was the epitome of compassion and consolation.

"Dylan," she began quietly, "you have to stop being so hard on yourself." As she said the words, it suddenly seemed as if the noisy crowd surrounding them melted away, leaving the two of them all alone.

"But I've just found out that I've been neglecting my daughter."

The passion and self-recrimination in his voice took her by surprise.

"You're going to change that." She filled the simple statement with all the confidence she could muster.

She *was* confident that he would change his behavior with Abbie. But it was evident from the look on his face that her trust in him wasn't enough to change how badly he felt about himself.

"Dylan, Abbie is a bright and healthy child," she told him. "She's inquisitive. She's outgoing. She's very self-assured. Mrs. Nichols loves her and takes good care of her. Your father loved her dearly, and from what I've heard about their trips to Dewey, he spent lots of time with Abbie.''

She squeezed Dylan's hand lightly. ''Abbie hasn't been neglected.''

He mumbled something unintelligible and, Laura guessed, self-critical.

She sighed. ''Now, I will agree that you haven't spent enough time with Abbie. But you love your daughter, I can see that.'' He searched her gaze, and she knew he appreciated her last comment.

''One good thing about being a parent,'' she continued, ''is that even though we can't fix our past mistakes with our kids, we can always try not to make those same mistakes again.''

The shadow of a smile hovered on his lips for a moment as he thought over what she'd said. Then his mouth pulled into a full, totally agreeing smile, and it was as though the bright, blazing sun had broken through thick, gray clouds. Laura felt her heart lighten and she returned a smile of her own. He understood what she'd been trying to tell him—that his preceding mistakes didn't matter, so long as he tried not to repeat them, and that it was the here and now that counted. He and Abbie were going to be okay. She felt sure of it, and that knowledge made her soul sing.

He turned his hand palm up and entwined his fingers with hers.

''Since you've come to Wilmington,'' he said, ''you've changed things.''

"Oh?" She couldn't keep the uncertainty out of her tone.

"For the better," he assured her.

"Oh," she said, and reddened at his compliment.

"I mean it." His head tilted to one side. "You've helped me with Abbie. And I can't tell you how ecstatic the employees are at Mitchell Corporation. The parents can't wait for the day-care center to open."

The excitement she felt about her project made her stomach giddy. Sliding back in her seat, she pulled her hand from his and didn't even try to fight the grin that overtook her face whenever she spoke about the new center.

"I'll be ready to open the doors soon," she happily announced. "I sent an electronic-mail message to all the parents who signed up their children, telling them that the day care will open a week from Monday."

"So soon?"

She nodded. "The painters are finished. The new carpet is laid. I've even done some hiring already. There was a young woman who came asking about a job last week. I don't know how she knew I was looking for applicants, I had just placed the advertisement. But she was very eager." Laura chuckled, remembering. "And very persistent. Her name is T.C. and she came to see me every day for three days straight."

He folded his hands on the armrest and listened intently.

Laura checked on the children with a quick glance and then turned back to Dylan.

"T.C.'s qualifications are a little weak," Laura admitted. "She hasn't kept a steady job since she finished her two-year degree."

Dylan frowned. "That can be a red flag when you're hiring new people. Anyone who can't hold on to a job—"

"But," Laura quickly interrupted, "what she lacks in credentials, she makes up for in sheer enthusiasm. And besides, I really like her. She gets along well with Brian."

"She's spent time with Brian?"

"Well...yes." Laura felt put on the spot. She couldn't understand his suspicious nature. "T.C. has been at the center for the past few days. She was so eager for a job, so enthusiastic to start that she offered to help me get things set up, and since I bring Brian in with me..." She let the thought trail, letting him put two and two together.

"What some people see as enthusiasm, might be deemed desperation by others."

Stunned by his blatant pessimism, she simply sat there and stared at him. Finally, she asked, "Why are you being so negative? You've never met this woman."

He reached out and enveloped her hand with his. "You're right. I am being negative, and it's not fair of me. I trust your judgment of this woman's character."

The honesty in his statement cleared away the clouds she felt hanging over them.

"You're sure?" she asked.

"Sure, I'm sure."

"Good." She grinned. "Because I want to borrow Abbie."

As quickly as the skeptical mask had been peeled from his face, it was now plastered back into place.

"What do you mean, you want to borrow Abbie?"

"Well, T.C. has her heart set on working with the younger children," Laura explained. "I've seen her with Brian, and she's very good. Nurturing, yet not smothering. Friendly, but doesn't come off as a buddy." Laura stopped, feeling the need to explain what she meant. "She expects to be respected, and she reciprocates that same behavior with Brian. Some people are too lenient with children and let them say and do whatever they wish. And then there are people who are so strict that they lose sight of the fact that children deserve just as much respect as adults. T.C. is somewhere in the middle. She's creative in her ideas for games. I really think she'll be a great asset to the day-care center. But like I said, she doesn't have any qualifications to work with the younger ones."

"So you want my Abbie to be a guinea pig."

"Oh, Dylan, please don't look at it that way. I'll be there every minute. I just want to see what kind of rapport T.C. can develop with a child younger than Brian."

Dylan studied her for a long, silent moment and Laura once again couldn't help but notice how sharp and predatory his dark gaze became when he donned his cloak of suspicion. He slipped into this distrustful nature so easily, sported the well-worn emotion so naturally that Laura suspected he didn't even realize when this dubious, watchful idiosyncrasy of his was showing.

As she watched him study her, she once again found herself wondering what had happened to him in the past to create this distrustful facet of his personality.

Finally, he spoke. "I trust you, Laura. And if you trust this T.C. with Brian...and if you like her...then she has to be okay." He smiled then. "I'll be happy to bring Abbie to the center next week."

Laura was surprised by the lightness and relief that flooded through her. She couldn't explain it, but for some silly reason she felt as if she'd acquired Dylan's approval, and that made her...happy.

"Look, Daddy." Abbie thrust a cardboard baseball card at Dylan. "Look what I got."

"Wow, honey," Dylan crooned to his daughter as he lifted her onto the seat next to him.

"Mom! Mom!" Brian came running up the concrete steps toward Laura. "Can you believe it? I got three cards! They're signed! This is great!"

Laura had to chuckle at her son's exuberance.

"It *is* great," she agreed.

Brian plunked himself into the aisle seat just as

the stadium announcer's voice began to boom over the loudspeaker to report the starting lineup.

The seventh-inning stretch was a long time in coming, and after hot dogs, French fries, soda pop, ice-cream bars and cotton candy, Dylan and Laura looked at each other and at their weary children and decided to call it a night.

Abbie was asleep when Dylan placed her in the back seat of the car and buckled her safety belt. Laura knew Brian's heavy eyes would probably close before Dylan could get the car onto the Interstate 95, and she was right.

The short drive home was filled with pleasant, easy conversation, and when Dylan parked the car, he turned to her.

"I've enjoyed myself so much," he said, "I hate to see the evening end."

Laura felt the same way. "Well...you could come over to the cottage." She turned to glance into the darkness of the backseat where the children were sleeping. "We can tuck Abbie in on the couch and—" Laura shrugged, a little self-conscious about the invitation "—we can sit on the porch for a while." Her eyes met his in the dim light of the car. "I have a nice bottle of white wine."

The smile he gave her caused her heart to flip over in her chest.

"I'd love that."

His words were soft, but the utter sincerity in his tone sent a tiny ripple coursing up her spine.

Dylan carried Abbie to the cottage. Laura offered to carry her son when he awakened, but Brian insisted with sleepy indignation that he could walk on his own.

She unlocked the front door and the four of them entered the cozy little living room.

"I'll take Brian to his room," Laura whispered to Dylan. "You can lay Abbie on the couch. There's a cotton blanket on the shelf in the closet, there."

Dylan nodded. "Good-night, Brian," he called softly before turning away from them.

Laura helped her son into his pajamas and then pulled back the sheet so he could slip into bed. Smoothing back the fine hair that tousled across his forehead, she planted a kiss on his soft skin.

"Good-night," she said, but she could tell from his deep, even breathing that he was already asleep.

As she closed the door to his room, she stood in the hall gazing toward the living room. She could see Dylan tucking back tendrils of Abbie's long, blond hair. He bent over and placed a soft kiss on the child's cheek. Laura's heart squeezed with warm emotion. Dylan was a wonderful father.

And he filled out those jeans quite nicely, too, she observed, and in an instant an unwitting image came to her mind—an image of firm, muscular thighs and calves, tanned skin completely free of blue jeans. Helplessly wrapped up in the thought, she found herself wondering what type of underwear he preferred, boxers or briefs. She blinked herself back to reality and felt her face flame hotly. She reached up to cover her mouth with her hand. Lord, but she was glad he didn't realize he was being watched—that he didn't know he was being thought about in such a...boldly erotic manner.

Despite the strange, tense undercurrent between them, her attraction for this man ran strong. She needed to take things slow. She hadn't been with a man since her husband had died so many long years ago. She hadn't felt the need for a man in her life, she hadn't felt the desire. Until now.

But she had no idea how Dylan felt about her. Well, she had some; his smile had been friendly enough, and his eyes... She'd thought those dark, piercing eyes of his had asked her silent, secret questions.

Laura nearly chuckled aloud. Silent, secret questions. She was being silly. What did she know about dating, relationships or man/woman allure? She could fit what she knew about men in a teacup, for heaven's sake.

What she did realize was that she'd better just sit back and let Dylan take the leading role. She was aware of her attraction toward him. Now, she needed to wait to see if he felt the same.

At that moment, Dylan happened to turn his head and look down the short hallway where she stood. Her smile was shaky, self-conscious after her quiet revelation, and she felt like a fool to have gotten lost in her thoughts as she studied him. She forcefully reminded herself that he had no idea how long she'd been standing there gawking.

She moved toward him on legs that were as pliable as warm jelly.

"I'll only be a minute," she said, veering off toward the kitchen.

She deftly uncorked the bottle of wine and then opened the cabinet where she kept the glasses. When she returned to the living room Dylan was standing by the front screen door.

"Let's go out in the yard," he suggested. "The sky is clear—" he gazed outside and then back at her "—and the stars are beautiful."

She nodded, helpless against the wave of excited anticipation that swept through her.

The night air was like silk as they made their way to the covered wooden swing that sat in the middle of the yard between the main house and the cottage.

"Since moving to Wilmington," Laura commented, "the only thing I miss about Dewey is my evening walk on the beach. It was breezy and refreshing, and the sound of the waves crashing on the shore..." She hesitated a moment, reminiscing. Then she chuckled, suddenly discomfited. "I'm sorry. I didn't mean...it's not that I don't like the city...."

"It's okay," he said. "I understand. Dewey was your home. It's okay to miss it. I just hope you're happy enough here to want to stay."

"Oh, I am," she assured him. "This day-care center is my dream. Your father knew that."

When they reached the swing, he took the wine bottle from her. "I'll do the honors," he said.

She smiled. "Please."

After she sat, she took the glass he offered. He placed the bottle on the grass next to the swing and then slid next to her, but not too close, she noticed.

He raised his glass. "To a wonderful day together," he toasted.

The glasses clinked together softly as she touched the rim of hers to his. He gazed at her as he sipped, and Laura felt the mood between them grow suddenly warm and…intimate. There was something in his eyes…something dark and mysterious that sent a delicious quiver up her spine. She felt the fine, wispy hairs at the base of her neck stand on end. And in that moment, she realized that he too—although he didn't say so in words—felt the same attraction for her that she felt for him.

It was a luscious revelation for her to realize that Dylan wanted her. It had been so many years since she'd felt…pretty. So many years since she'd been the object of a man's desire. And desire was exactly what Dylan was feeling. She could read it in his gaze, see it in the set of his jaw, and it caused a tiny tingle of apprehension to tickle her belly. And it grew more intense with each passing second.

She sipped at her wine and felt its satiny warmth as it slid over her tongue and down her throat. Honesty about the anxiety coiling inside her was on her lips before she realized it as she softly admitted, ''I haven't felt this way in a very long time.''

She knew that he knew exactly to what she was referring as he stared, silently, intently, and acute embarrassment made her lower her gaze. Maybe honesty wasn't the best idea, after all. Maybe she'd misread the signals she'd thought he'd sent her. Maybe—

''Me either.''

His quiet words sounded stentorian in the tranquil night, or maybe it was just that she'd been holding her breath as she waited for his reaction to her words. Her breath left her in a rush—she hated all this second guessing herself and her thoughts. But then, wasn't that what the beginning of a more intimate relationship was all about?

The unbidden question startled her. Was that what this was? The beginning of a more intimate relationship? How could she not have realized it before? The tiny tingle of apprehension she'd felt a moment before flared into a hot flame of fear.

He lowered his glass and enveloped her fingers in his. ''You're trembling.''

His voice was as warm and soothing as his hand on hers. His grip tightened the smallest bit.

''Laura,'' he began, ''we're both adults here. This thing can go as fast or as slow as we choose.''

He couldn't possibly know how grateful she felt hearing those words. The panic that had been steadily rising inside her subsided to a quiet, tolerable pulsing. He acknowledged the attraction between them, yet gave her the space he obviously recognized she felt in desperate need of.

But why had this need for distance suddenly flared? she wondered. Why couldn't she simply act on the emotions and the attraction she felt for Dylan?

Honesty once more prevailed, for as the explanation tumbled about in her mind, it tumbled from her mouth.

"I married my high-school sweetheart," she found herself saying. "Tom and I were so young." She gave a small smile. "So young..." She raised her eyes to Dylan's. "I loved Brian's father. I have some wonderful memories of our marriage."

It seemed the most natural thing in the world to admit this to Dylan. And he didn't seem the least bit upset or put off by her candor.

"What happened to him?" Dylan asked.

The sincerity in his question told Laura unequivocally that he wasn't threatened by her memories of her first marriage, and that pleased her because she refused to feel ashamed of the happy years she'd spent with her husband. She didn't want to be involved with a man whose self-confidence would be diminished by the grief she felt over Tom's death. Yes, her sorrow had diminished over the years, but that didn't change the fact that she had felt it. She was relieved to realize that Dylan wouldn't be affected by her comfortable, content past.

"He was diagnosed with cancer," she told Dylan.

"The doctors did everything they could, but..." She let the explanation drift. It was enough.

"I'm sorry. But I'm glad you have such wonderful memories."

Again, Laura was touched by his utter sincerity. She sent him a grateful smile.

"Tell me about Abbie's mother," she prompted.

Like lightning from the blue, his gentle countenance hardened, taking her by surprise. The bitterness that glittered in his eyes astounded her, and the acidic mask of anger that slid so quickly into place made her straighten her spine and inch away from him.

"You don't want to know." The short sentence was curt and to the point.

Laura was at a loss for something to say. She hadn't meant to stir unpleasant memories, she'd only wished to know more about him.

It was as if he read her thoughts. He sighed, and the hardness left his gaze.

"I'm sorry," he said, entwining her fingers with his. "I wouldn't mind telling you about Teresa." He halted, then looked directly in her eyes as he continued, "It's just that I don't want to unload on you when things between us are so...new."

So, Laura thought, *he has some not-so-pleasant memories.* Could these memories have anything to do with why he was always so defensive? So wary? She felt certain of it, and her curiosity was roused.

But she tamped it down. He'd tell her when he was ready. Until then, she'd simply have to wait.

He moved closer to her. "Tonight, I'd just like to enjoy the night." He looked up into the black, velvet sky. "I'd like to enjoy this delicious wine."

When he took a sip, she was compelled to do the same. Then he took the glass from her, placed them both on the ground next to the bottle and turned back to her.

"And I'd like to enjoy your company."

He slid his arm across the back of the swing, and she could feel the heat of his skin through the thin material of her blouse. She looked at him, so close, so inviting, and couldn't keep her eyes from roving to his perfectly shaped mouth. She took a split second to dream what it would be like to feel his lips on hers. Hoped against hope that maybe…just maybe…

Suddenly there was no doubt in her mind that he was going to kiss her.

Chapter Four

The first touch of his lips on hers was gentle, almost tentative, as though he was measuring her reaction to this initial seductive invasion. His mouth barely brushed against hers before he pulled back a fraction, and Laura knew what true disappointment was.

She felt his fingers entwine in her hair and slide softly along the nape of her neck. With his other hand, he smoothed his knuckles along her jaw.

"You're beautiful," he whispered.

A delicious thrill rippled through her.

He buried his nose in her hair and she heard him inhale deeply. Then, unexpectedly, he gave the tiniest groan and nibbled on the lobe of her ear, then moved on down along her neck.

Sensory perceptions bombarded her brain: the reverberation of pleasure emanating from deep in his chest; the sound of his breathing; the sweet smells of the summer night mingling with the scent of his skin all clean and warm and…male; the sight of his dark, dark hair against the even darker sky; the feel of his hands on her skin; the texture of his rough, whisker-stubbled jaw against her cheek; the vibration from the pounding of his heart—or was it hers? The only one of her senses left wanting was that of taste, and it screamed out to her unrelentingly.

Placing her hand on the side of his face, she made a move to draw his lips to hers, to satisfy the urge to taste him. But he chose that moment to gingerly rake his teeth on the sensitive area directly behind her ear, and then he soothed the spot with the hot velvet of his tongue.

Laura stifled the moan that threatened to escape from her throat, and she was overwhelmed by some basic, primitive response that had, before this moment, been repressed somewhere deep in the recesses of her brain. If there had been time to think, she'd have been shocked by the erotic desire welling within her. But she hadn't time to think—only time to react.

Her inhalation was shaky as she dragged his mouth to hers. In her desperation to taste his kiss, she tugged on the material of his shirt, nearly whimpering with the frantic need to feel.

His second assault on her mouth was just that— an assault. And it was just what Laura wanted. His lips were moist and firm, their pressure intense, and she felt utterly wanton as she relented to the impulse to skim her tongue lightly along them.

His audible groan sent goose bumps racing over her skin. When his lips parted, she felt the silky heat of his tongue, tasted the warm, tangy essence of wine. Her mind whirled with an overpowering desire to get closer, ever closer to him.

Sliding her arms under his, she splayed both hands on his broad back and pulled him tight to her. She was in heaven. The feel of his solidness against her was pure paradise.

Dylan felt Laura's breasts press, firm and snug, against his chest, felt her fingertips dig into his back, realized the raw desire the two of them had unleashed, and he broke off the kiss. He had to.

His lips were a scant inch from her delicate, white ear, his tone coming in a ragged whisper as he pleaded, "Laura."

Gulping in oxygen, he tried hard to get a grip on the riotous emotions that were urging him to further this intimacy, compelling him to do things he knew she was not ready for. Hell, he didn't know if he was ready, either.

He wanted desperately to pull her onto his lap. But he couldn't, because then she'd know, exactly and literally, just how much he ached for her. He wanted to cup his hands around her breasts, feel the weight of them in his palms. But he wouldn't let himself, couldn't let himself, because he just might lose the already tenuous hold he had on restraint.

He leaned back and gazed at her face. She lowered her eyes shyly and he felt a tug deep in his gut at the demure gesture. The moon threw shadows over the delicate planes of her features. She was so beautiful. And not just on the outside. She'd helped him tremendously since her arrival. This was one special woman.

Curling his index finger under her chin, he tipped up her head just enough so that she was forced to look at him. Her blue eyes were nearly navy in the pearlescent darkness of night. The color was soft and more than appealing, and he could clearly read the desire she was feeling for him.

At the very idea that she wanted him, he felt himself tighten with a deep, barely restrained craving. Dear God, he would die from this hunger!

"I'm sorry."

Her voice was barely a whisper on the still summer air. Her apology bewildered him.

"For what?" he asked softly.

She tried to turn from him, but he again captured her chin in his fingers.

"Please," he prompted. "I want to know what you're thinking."

She swallowed and he resisted the urge to trace his finger down the length of her elegant throat, feel the smoothness of her creamy skin.

"I feel like I've…"

She hesitated and her eyes turned sooty with timidity, but the desire never escaped their deep blue depths. Dylan thought it was a wondrous combination.

"...been too...forward," she murmured.

His insides compressed with an odd squeezing sensation. "Oh, no," he told her. "That's not true."

She studied his face as she absently smoothed her hand over the material of his shirtfront that had been wrinkled by her grip. Finally she gave him a sad smile.

"I think I was," she said. "Otherwise, why did you...why did we..." Her cheeks colored endearingly. "Why did you stop kissing me?"

The blunt question threw him. He wasn't ready for it and found himself speechless for a moment.

She turned her whole body away from him on the wooden seat. "I *was* too forward," she stated. "I assumed—"

"You're wrong, Laura." Sliding close, he enveloped her in his arms. He pulled her back against his chest and rested his jaw on her flower-scented hair and marveled at the silky thickness of it. "I wanted that just as much as you did. I had to stop."

He placed his hands on her shoulders and slowly turned her around to face him. "Don't you see?" His head tilted with the strength of his emotion. "I wanted you so much, I *had* to stop."

Dylan hoped she understood his totally inadequate explanation. He held his breath waiting for her response.

When she finally spoke, her voice was husky with

feeling. "The...feelings I had were so strong," she said. "I've never felt anything like that before. I was surprised...I was...overwhelmed."

He couldn't help but smile at her honesty. And, cradling her face between his hands, he looked deeply into her eyes. "Me too," he said.

One corner of her mouth tipped upward and he knew she didn't realize how sexy the movement was.

"I'm glad," she told him, and then she turned her body around and leaned into him.

Sitting there with her back resting against his chest, her head nestled in the crook of his neck, they gazed at the stars, and Dylan was certain she could feel the steady hammering of his heart. And he was glad.

"'Bye, Tracy," Laura brightly called from the doorway. She waved at the little girl.

A young boy was just leaving the day-care center with his father, a man who worked in the research division of Mitchell Corporation.

"See you tomorrow, Mark." Laura smiled and handed him his yellow lunch box.

"This day-care center was a great idea, Ms. Adams," the boy's father remarked. "This makes life so much easier on both me and my wife. And Mark looks forward to coming. It was great to pop in and have lunch with him." He grinned before continuing, "I know it's early to form an opinion after only a week, but I'm very happy with the new facility."

"I'm glad," Laura replied. "That's what it's all about." She gave Mark one final wave goodbye. "I'll see you on Monday," she called.

Turning toward the now empty playroom, Laura heaved a contented sigh. The vivid primary colors of the walls were cheery in the afternoon sunlight. The room was neat; all the toys were in their appropriate bins, the dress-up clothes hung on pegs. A slow, sanguine smile crept across her mouth. Again she sighed and combed her fingers through her hair, sweeping it back from her face.

Granted, she was exhausted after the center's first full week, but it was a wonderful weariness. Things couldn't have gone more perfectly than they had. All seven women and the one young man she'd hired as care-givers showed up on time each morning. Laura had hired a sufficient number of people so that she could act as a "floater"—someone to "float" between the rooms and help out wherever she was needed. Yes, things *had* gone perfectly this week, or almost perfectly. There was one little problem—a problem she was certain she could straighten out by just talking to T.C. And she'd do that before leaving today.

She chuckled softly to think how the children insisted on calling the adults in charge "teacher." All week long, Laura had heard a litany of, "Teacher, I'm thirsty, Teacher, I have to go to the bathroom, Teacher, when do we get to play outside?"

The people she'd hired didn't have teaching credentials, yet they were not mere baby-sitters either. The "teachers" were responsible for planning educational games to expand the minds of the children, and they organized physical activities to help in building strong bodies. Laura knew a day-care center couldn't ever be the perfect environment for children—being a parent herself, she realized the best place for a child was being cared for by mom or dad. But just short of that, she wanted the center to be a healthy, happy situation for the children in her charge.

Laura left the large, open room that she'd designated as the community playroom and went down the small hallway that led to the classrooms and her office. As she passed the open doorways, she saw her employees tidying up and making preparations for Monday. Entering her office, she reached for the stack of white envelopes that held the paychecks. A tiny flashing light on her computer terminal caught her eye, alerting her that an electronic-mail message was awaiting her attention.

She sat down and pushed the button that would call the message to her screen. The note was from Dylan, as she knew it would be, and it was addressed not only to her but to at least two dozen other Mitchell Corporation employees. She'd been receiving these mass electronic mailings from him all week, and from them she'd learned that Dylan and his researchers were on to something very big, something very secretive.

Reading the impersonal message, Laura felt a sudden flash of disappointment wash over her. Oh, she was happy that Dylan was on the verge of some new and exciting business success. But she was so disillusioned by the fact that he'd so easily slipped back into his workaholic routine. Especially after he'd promised to change just two short weeks ago.

She eased back against her chair and stared out the window, not really seeing the shiny, new playground equipment that had been installed in the center's fenced-in play area.

Her thoughts went back to the weekend before last when Dylan had taken her and Brian and Abbie to see the Blue Rocks play baseball. And, before she realized it, images began to bombard her brain—images of their time alone together that same night under the stars. His hands on her skin. The warm, male scent of him enfolding her, drugging her senses. His mouth on her neck, her ear, her lips. It had been a deliriously wonderful evening. And it had only been the beginning....

Laura let her mind rove over the late afternoons that she and Dylan, Brian and Abbie had spent together. The home-cooked meals she'd made for them had been eaten with lots of cheery conversation and laughter. And, oh, the times they'd spent alone together, just the two of them after the children had been tucked safely into bed; warm, starlit nights, intimate talks, hot passionate kisses. The memories those nights had given her made her heart race.

But then things had changed. There had been some sort of breakthrough in this new project Dylan had been working on—

The knock on her open door made her jerk to attention.

"Oh, T.C.," she stammered, straightening in her seat and shoving her hand through her hair. "Come in, come right in...."

The young woman tilted her head. "I didn't mean to startle you." Then her perky mouth shifted into an impish grin. "You were deep in thought. And your eyes were all misty. Were you thinking of a man?"

Laura chuckled. "Guilty as charged," she admitted. She'd spent quite a bit of time getting to know T.C. over the past couple of weeks, and she felt close enough to this woman that she didn't give the confession a second thought. Then the smile faded from her face. "But I'm a little upset with him. He's been kind of busy with his work and hasn't called me all week."

Nor has he come to the center once, she thought. *Nor has he spent time with his daughter.* But she didn't need to dump all her discontent on T.C.

"That's too bad," T.C. said. "If you want to talk..."

Laura looked at the young woman's sincere expression of concern and felt T.C.'s offer to listen to her problem was a sweet gesture.

"Well, thanks," Laura said, "but I'm sure I'll see him over the weekend. We'll work things out."

"I'm glad." T.C.'s cap of silky blond hair swung as she gave an animated nod. She pointed at the envelopes Laura still held in her grasp. "May I?" she asked.

"Of course," Laura said, searching for and then handing over T.C.'s paycheck.

"I can't tell you how much I need this."

While T.C. ripped open the envelope and perused the check, Laura utilized the moment to study the woman. Her face was free of makeup, giving her youthful countenance a freshness that could easily be described as beautiful. Her earnestness had captured Laura's heart from day one, and the young woman's large blue eyes were like a window that expressed her every emotion. T.C. was timid and seemed... lonely.

Laura was hesitant to bring up the problem she'd noticed this week in T.C.'s classroom. She liked this woman. And didn't want to hurt her by criticizing. But T.C. was an employee of the center, and her behavior had a direct impact on the day care's success. Besides, the children were also affected by her actions, and that alone was enough to make Laura speak up.

"I'm glad you stopped in," Laura began softly. "I wanted to talk to you before you left for the day."

"What?" T.C. immediately became alarmed.

"What have I done? You're not going to fire me, are you?"

Laura couldn't hold back her chuckle. "Of course not," she said. "But I have witnessed a problem. But, I'm sure that when we talk about it, we'll be able to straighten everything out."

T.C. lowered herself into the chair in the corner. "What have I done, Laura?"

The anxiety on T.C.'s face tore at Laura's heart. She wanted so badly to comfort T.C., to tell her that it was okay. But she was the boss, and she had to confront the issue.

Laura folded her hands on the desk, and tried to conjure a professional expression. She knew she failed, though, because T.C. wasn't just an employee—she'd become a friend.

Her smile was gentle. "I know that you've spent more time with Abbie than you have the other children..." She hesitated, searching for kind words for what needed to be said. "The bond the two of you share is only natural since you spent that extra week together, just the two of you."

"Abbie's a special little girl." T.C.'s tone was soft and utterly honest.

So is her father. The thought came to her mind automatically, and with it came a crystal-clear image of Dylan's dark, piercing eyes, his handsome, chiseled features. She would have loved to dwell on it, to savor the picture in her head, but she knew this was not the time and felt the need to force it from her.

"Abbie *is* special," Laura agreed. "But so are the other six children in that room."

"But—"

"No buts, T.C.," Laura insisted. "There can be no favoritism shown while you're working for Mitchell Corporation. None."

T.C.'s gaze lowered guiltily.

"You're going to feel partiality," Laura stressed. "It's going to happen. You care for a child who resembles you when you were young. Or you care for a child who is the spitting image of some relative. Or...or...has eyes that reminds you of your own child..." She tilted her head to one side as she continued tenderly, "I'm not saying you have to keep yourself from feeling it. That would be impossible. But I am saying that you have to keep yourself from *showing* it."

There was a long moment of silence as Laura waited for T.C.'s reaction. She knew from a full week of observation that T.C. was emotionally attached to Abbie. Understanding that this was T.C.'s first job working with children, Laura sympathized with her.

Finally, T.C. looked directly into Laura's eyes and nodded slowly.

"You're right," she said, her voice soft as a whisper. "I've shown some favoritism where Abbie's concerned. I won't let it happen again. I'll be more attentive to the other children. I promise.''

Laura smiled.

"You're not angry at me, are you?" T.C. asked.

"I'm not angry. And I'm sure you'll do the right thing. I know you're the right person for this job." Laura grinned, and hoping to dispel the solemn mood that had settled over them, she added, "*I* hired you, didn't I?"

T.C.'s full mouth curled into a small smile. "Yeah, you did."

"And I *am* the expert, aren't I?"

This question made T.C. actually chuckle. "Yeah," she said. "You are."

Laura stood and leaned her hip against the edge of the desk. "So, get out of here, enjoy your weekend and I'll see you bright and early on Monday."

After saying her goodbyes to T.C., Laura delivered the other employees' paychecks, and after they left for the day, she locked up the day care and headed for the parking lot.

Driving home through busy rush-hour traffic, she thought of T.C. and Abbie. It was no wonder that Abbie would cling to T.C. Abbie was an affectionate child and easily became attached to anyone who showed her some loving attention. She'd seen Abbie cleave to Brian. And Mrs. Nichols. Abbie was a child looking for love.

Laura frowned as her next thought came barreling into her brain. *It should be Dylan who gives Abbie the love she's seeking. Not some teacher in a day-care center.*

"I have to talk to Dylan," she decided aloud. "I have to."

She pulled into the winding drive, steered the car around the big house and parked her four-door compact in the garage next to Dylan's sleek, black sports car. She was surprised that he was home from work so early. He'd been staying until after dark all week. As she crossed the yard, the sound of childish laughter caught her attention, making her smile. Abbie had begged for Brian to be able to come home with her when Mrs. Nichols had picked her up at the end of the day, and Laura had been happy to let Brian go.

Veering toward the side yard where she knew Abbie had a sandbox and a tree swing, Laura rounded some bushy shrubs and called a hello to Abbie and her son, both of whom sat at a wooden picnic table.

"Hi, Mom," Brian said, picking up a bright red crayon.

Abbie was bent over her piece of drawing paper, so intent on creating her picture that her tongue poked from between her pursed lips.

"Hi, kids." Laura ruffled her son's mop of dark hair and made a mental note to take him to the barber.

When Abbie didn't respond, she looked closer at the image the child was so focused on drawing. Laura could make out a circle with an egg shape underneath it. She watched as Abbie added two stick-like legs and short, flat lines for feet.

"That's a beautiful picture, Abbie," she said.

"It's smudged," the little girl complained.

"She got some chocolate on it from a chocolate-chip cookie," Brian chimed in. "But I told her it didn't matter. That she was still doin' good."

"She is," Laura agreed. Then, as Abbie added stick arms, Laura asked, "Who are you drawing?"

Excitement twinkled in Abbie's eyes. "It's a secret."

Brian's chin tipped up as he gazed at Laura. "It's her new mom," he whispered.

Laura's initial reaction to hearing Abbie's secret wish was to think it pitiful and somehow forlorn, and an instant of sadness flared inside her. But then Abbie glared at Brian, her face indignant and angry.

"Brian," Abbie huffed, "that was a secret!"

Instantly contrite, Brian quickly said, "I'm sorry, Abbie. Mom won't tell. Will you, Mom?"

Abbie looked at her and Laura could clearly read the child's desperation.

"Don't tell daddy I told you, okay, Laura?" she pleaded.

Laura's heart raced and a euphoria washed over her strong enough to cause her skin to prickle all over. Blood rushed to her head, causing a whooshing sound that drowned out the normal everyday noises. Had Dylan talked to Abbie about a "new mom"? Had he discussed with his daughter the possibility of the four of them—Dylan, Abbie, Laura and Brian—coming together in a new family unit?

She knew that her and Dylan's feelings for one another ran deep, that the physical attraction they felt was nearly overwhelming at times. But…but could Dylan actually be thinking of…marriage? After knowing her only a couple of weeks?

"Stranger things have happened," she murmured, realizing that her feelings for him were strong enough that, if he did offer, she'd seriously consider it.

"Stranger than what, Mom?"

Brian's bewildered question snapped Laura back to the present and she looked down at the children.

"Oh, nothing, hon," she told him, giving his shoulder a pat. Then she directed her gaze at Abbie. "Don't you worry. I won't tell your dad that I know about the secret."

Abbie's smile came easily and was instantly trusting. Then she dipped her head and focused once again on her unfinished work of art.

"I saw your dad's car in the garage," Laura observed. "Is he inside?"

Without looking up, Abbie said, "Locked up tight in his study."

Laura smiled, knowing that Abbie had to be mimicking Mrs. Nichols's words.

"Brian, I'll start dinner in a few minutes," she said.

"Can we go out for pizza?"

She gazed into her son's expectant face. "Sure," she told him. "I just need to have a few words with Dylan first and then we'll go."

As she walked across the lawn toward the big house, Laura's insides turned heavy as lead. She felt as though she was on her way to scold a wayward child. Dylan was a grown man, and she doubted that he'd appreciate being reprimanded.

But she couldn't stand by and say nothing. She had to bring this problem to his attention, seeing as how she was his friend.... That thought brought to her mind Abbie's secret of a new mom. It seemed as though Laura was becoming more than just a friend to Dylan. Much more.

When she again pointed out to him that he was working too much, would he see it as nagging? she wondered. And would that change the way he felt about her?

She lifted her chin determinedly, feeling the need to be true to Alfred's memory. Alfred wanted his son and his granddaughter to have a wonderful, close relationship. Laura simply had to talk to Dylan. For Abbie's sake. And for his.

Mrs. Nichols's usually smiling face was solemn when she answered Laura's knock.

"He's working, Laura," the older woman said.

"Well, I really need to speak to him," she replied.

"He's working—"

"He works too much." Laura slipped around Mrs. Nichols and started down the hall.

Mrs. Nichols turned toward the kitchen muttering something to the tune of, "It's impossible to change a man."

Her confrontation with the housekeeper only made the lead in her chest grow heavier. She really didn't relish the idea of having words with Dylan. She would rather have had things between them remain...friendly. No, that wasn't the right word. Affectionate, that was more like it. And she smiled. Immediately another word came to mind.... Passionate. *Yes,* she thought, her smile returning, *that's how I'd like things to remain.*

Suddenly, she found herself at the closed door of Dylan's study. And the leaden feeling increased tenfold. She knew she had to do this. She simply had to.

She knocked and turned the knob when he called, "Come in."

The sight of him bent over some papers on his desk nearly took her breath away. His handsome features, those black eyes, his even blacker hair. His shirt-sleeves were rolled up, exposing his taut, muscular forearms. And those hands. The only word to describe them was...sexy.

He looked up, and she felt she couldn't take a breath. Then he smiled, and she was certain she was lost. How could she talk to him when she couldn't even breathe? she wondered. She'd have to find a way.

"Hi." The crease of concentration in his brow

softened at the sight of her, as did the tension around his mouth. "I was going to call you this evening."

"You were?" She barely got the words out in a hoarse whisper. She hadn't realized just how much she'd missed him this week.

He stood, came around his desk and crossed the room to her. When he enfolded her in his arms, Laura was taken completely by surprise. Without thought she wrapped her arms around his waist.

"I've missed you," she found herself saying, and she laid her head against his broad chest. He smelled so good...felt so wonderful.

He kissed the top of her head and she lifted her face, offering him her lips. He didn't disappoint her.

His kiss was hungry and fierce, and Laura matched it with a shocking intensity.

Then, like a cold douse of water on the growing embers of a flame, she remembered her mission.

"Dylan," she murmured against his lips.

He pulled back and gazed at her, desire evident in his onyx eyes.

"I need to talk to you."

"I have some things to say to you, too," he said. "I know that I kind of broke my word about work this week. But we're on to something, Laura. Something big. And I needed to be at the office. But I want you to know that I've spent time with Abbie. I've tucked her into bed every night. I've read her stories and talked to her about her experiences at the day care." He smiled down at her. "I have been careful to be a good father to Abbie. And it's just about over. I shouldn't have to be at the office so much next week.''

Laura pulled him tighter, happy about all the things that he'd said. There really wasn't a problem where Abbie was concerned. He was making every effort to spend time with his daughter.

''It's you I'm worried about,'' he continued.

She frowned. ''What do you mean?'' she asked. ''Why are you worried about me?''

''I feel like I've neglected you. I haven't called. I haven't come to see how things are going at the center. I've just been—''

She reached up and placed her silencing fingers softly against his lips.

''Don't,'' she told him. ''Don't worry.''

He held her close and she absorbed the over-whelmingly intimate emotions emanating from him as though she were a dry sponge.

Finally, he looked down at her. ''So, what did you come to see me about?''

She was quiet for a moment. She had been so worried about a confrontation with Dylan, and all along there hadn't even been a problem. There was no reason at all for her to complain about the long hours he'd worked this past week. That would only cause him to feel bad all over again.

Hugging him tight, she murmured against his chest, ''I've just been feeling neglected.''

He placed those sexy hands of his on either side of her face and gazed directly into her eyes.

"We'll have to fix that then, won't we?" he asked, his voice gravelly with the desire he so obviously felt for her.

She could only nod.

Chapter Five

"Is everything okay in here?" Laura leaned into the open doorway of T.C.'s room at the day-care center. The group of four-year-olds were seated around a rectangular table and the children were taking turns pouring themselves juice from a small pitcher. Laura smiled, knowing that this exercise would develop hand-eye coordination. The room was a riot of lunchtime noise: the crinkling of paper lunch bags, chairs scraping across the tile floor and the spirited, high-pitched chatter only children can make.

"We're doing just fine," T.C. said.

"I'm having lunch with Brian today." Laura waved a cheery hello to one little boy who had called out to her, and she was pleased to see the boy's mother had come in to have lunch with her son, as had several other parents.

"I'll stop back in around one, T.C."

"Okay, Laura."

Laura walked down the hallway and was so happy with her life, so delighted with the day-care center, so tickled with the world in general that she felt the urge to whistle, or sing, or give a joyous shout.

The weekend had been wonderful. Better than wonderful, if that was possible. Dylan had been attentive—to Abbie, to Brian, to Laura. Especially to Laura. It was as though the previous week, when he hadn't had time to call, when he'd worked so very hard, hadn't happened at all.

Dylan had been so interested to hear all about the day-care center's first week in operation, and she'd been happy to fill him in. He'd confided in her regarding the top-secret project he'd been developing with the help of his computer research technicians. She hadn't understood much of the jargon he'd used: bits and bytes, processors and megahertz, tape drives, imbedded keypads. But it didn't seem to matter that she didn't know much about what he spoke of; what had been important was that she'd seen his excitement and found herself wrapped up in it. She'd enjoyed hearing about his success.

Saturday evening he'd taken her to dinner—without the children. And it had been the most romantic evening of her life! They'd eaten at the classy and popular Hotel DuPont and then they had strolled along the Brandywine River.

He'd wooed her with tender words. He'd teased

her with sexy glances. He'd tempted her with soft, sensual kisses. And Laura had loved his undivided attention. But she'd been continually distracted by little Abbie's secret—the secret Abbie had begged her not to reveal. As the evening wore on, Laura felt as if she were focusing on it obsessively. Did Dylan really have in mind that they'd be a family? She'd thought about it so much that she felt certain she would just blurt out the secret and ruin everything.

But she hadn't. Somehow, she'd found the fortitude to remain calm—and silent. But, Lord, how she'd enjoyed his kisses.

To get to her son's room at the center she had to walk through the community playroom where the main door of the day care was located. She glanced at the heavy glass door as she went by and stopped short, a grin tugging at her mouth.

"Speak of the devil," she said.

Dylan let the door whisk closed behind him, his brows raised wickedly. "The devil?" he asked with mock innocence.

"Himself." The smile she bestowed on him was the definition of flirtation—pure and unadulterated.

She sauntered up to him—yes, sauntered—and she refused to apologize to anyone for it. She wanted this man and she wanted him to know it.

When she was within arm's reach, she stopped. "Hi, there," she murmured softly.

"Hi, yourself."

His voice was like satin sliding across her skin, and it made her tingle all over.

"If we were anywhere but here," she told him, "I'd kiss you."

His brows rose again and she could tell from the look on his handsome face that he was pleased.

"I would have liked that very much," he said, his tone husky.

They stood there, silently staring, enjoying the thick air of seduction that seemed to surround them.

Finally, when she could stand it no longer, she spoke.

"You came to see Abbie?"

He nodded. "I thought I'd share a glass of chocolate milk."

Laura smiled. "It's orange juice today."

"Mmmmm, my favorite."

There was something in his eyes that told her it wasn't orange juice at all that he was talking about, and she flushed with pleasure. She wanted to reach out to him, but didn't dare, afraid that she might lose her self-control and give in to her desire to smooth her fingers down his jaw, to feel the tautness of his muscled shoulders under her palms...

"You can find the four-year-olds down there." She pointed down the hallway behind her, knowing that if she didn't separate herself from him this instant, she just might give in to temptation. "They're a rowdy group, you can't miss them."

He smiled at her and she watched him cross the

playroom. The soft gray business suit fit his muscular form so well, and Laura stared even after he'd disappeared, taking a moment to quell her wildly thumping heart. Her feelings for Dylan were so strong it amazed her.

She made to turn away, but stopped short when she saw him poke his head around the corner.

"Hey," he called softly.

She remained silent, only raising her brows in question.

"Can you meet me in your office after lunch?"

A sultry promise twinkled in his black-as-night gaze, making Laura flush with pleasure. Helpless against the slow smile that tugged at her mouth, she simply nodded. He winked and was gone.

Inhaling deeply, she tried to calm her jittery nerves. She hurried to Brian's room, barely able to stifle the urge to skip. She couldn't wait until lunch was over!

The group of six-year-olds was more sedate and much quieter than the noisy toddlers in T.C.'s room. Laura greeted Maggie, the eldest member of her staff. Maggie had come out of retirement when she applied for a job as a care-giver at the center. The woman had told Laura that she simply had to find work—that doing nothing was going to kill her with boredom. Laura had liked the energetic senior citizen and thought she'd be a good addition to her day-care team. So far, Laura had been proven right. The children loved Maggie.

Sneaking up behind her son, Laura leaned over and planted a quick kiss on his cheek.

"Aw, Mom," he scolded, turning beet red.

"What's for lunch?" she asked. She slid out a child-sized chair and sat.

"You know," Brian said. "You packed the sandwiches this morning."

Just as she reached out for the pitcher of orange juice, Laura heard a commotion coming from the other side of the day care. She stopped in midmotion, frowning. Then she heard a child begin to wail, and she was out of her seat and through the door in an instant.

"Keep the children here, Maggie," Laura called over her shoulder.

Instinctively, she knew it was Abbie she heard crying and Laura ran across the playroom and down the hallway. She nearly careened into Dylan on his way out the door, tugging his reluctant, sobbing daughter behind him.

"You are to stay away from my daughter!"

The anger in Dylan's voice frightened Laura. The fury on his face scared her even more.

"What's—"

But she couldn't get her question out as the turbulent scene unfolded before her. T.C., looking scared as a bunny rabbit, was pleading with Dylan not to do this thing—whatever it was he was about to do. And Dylan's voice became louder with every word he threw at T.C.

"What the hell do you think you're doing? You are breaking the terms of our agreement."

Through a haze of confusion, Laura realized that several of the other four-year-olds were becoming upset by this angry situation. The parents who were present looked uncomfortable as well.

"Dylan." She reached out and placed a calming hand on his sleeve.

He jerked away from her as though her touch were a white-hot flame. His face contorted with the anger he directed at her. "What were you thinking to do this?" he shouted.

Her face drained of all color and her knees grew weak from the rage in his eyes. Why was he so very angry? What had happened to—

The thought broke off, but her mind continued to whirl with unanswered questions. Through the confusion, Laura noticed that the parents who watched were no longer uncomfortable—they were annoyed that their children were being allowed to witness this awful display. It was easy to prioritize her responsibilities here—her first concern was for the children.

"Dylan," she said, keeping her tone firm and inflexible, "let's go into my office and talk."

"I'm not going anywhere with you!"

The blind rage emanating from him literally took her breath away. She moved back a step as she tried to figure out what was going on and why Dylan was so angry.

"I'm taking my daughter out of here," he stated,

his voice now flat and quivering with barely suppressed emotion. "And she won't be coming back."

"Dylan, please!" T.C. begged. She broke down and began to sob uncontrollably.

"Will someone *please* explain what is going on?" Laura's question was released in a husky voice, and she ran agitated fingers through her hair. "Dylan, wait," she called, but he had already reached the corner and disappeared.

Then she heard Abbie's mewing little voice wail out, "Mommy!" before the door of the day-care center whooshed closed behind them.

Laura literally felt her face go ashen and she looked at T.C. A deep frown planted itself in her brow and she searched the young woman's eyes. Could what she was thinking be true? she wondered. Could T.C. really be—

The Mitchell Corporation employee who had come to have lunch with her son stepped forward, clearing her throat.

"Excuse me," she said softly. "But Billy is so upset. Is there any way that we can…"

The fog in Laura's brain cleared just enough so that she was able to put herself on autopilot. This was *her* day care. These children were *her* responsibility.

"T.C., I'll take over here for you," she said. "You go into my office until you can get yourself together." As she gave instructions, her voice grew stronger, less bewildered. "When you've calmed down, wash your face and come back. And then I'll go talk to Dylan.'' She was making her own plans out loud as she went along. ''We can fix this. Whatever it is.'' She patted T.C.'s forearm. ''Go on, now. It'll be okay.''

T.C. continued to cry softly as she went down the hallway.

Laura turned her attention to the group of frightened children.

''I'm sorry, everybody,'' she said, forcing a calmness into her tone that she certainly didn't feel. ''Let's all sit down and try to enjoy our lunch.''

''Why was Abbie crying?'' one little girl asked.

''How come our teacher left?'' another child lamented.

''Abbie's my friend,'' the first little girl said. ''Is she going to be here tomorrow?''

Laura answered the questions as honestly as she could without having all the answers herself. Naturally, the children were concerned and needed to talk about what they had witnessed.

Finally, she promised, ''I'm going to work this out with Abbie's father. I don't want you to worry. Everything's going to be okay.'' That seemed to relax them a little, and in an effort to calm them more, she suggested, ''How about if I read a story? Does anyone have a favorite?''

Billy's hand shot up and he retrieved a funny, rhyming story from the shelf. The children finished up their lunches and the parents who stopped in said

their goodbyes. Laura promised to talk separately
with the adults at a later date.

After the story, she got the children busy with finger paints and the next hour progressed as normally
as possible. When one of the children asked to hang
her picture to dry, Laura pinned the paper up onto
the bulletin board. A picture already hanging there
looked vaguely familiar and she took a second to
study it. The rounded face, the egg-shaped body, the
stick arms and legs. The corner was smudged with
chocolate. This was the picture Abbie had been
drawing at the picnic table when Brian had mistak-
enly revealed the little girl's secret.

Laura's stomach felt tight and achy. Tears blurred
her vision. She had so wanted to believe that the
"new mommy" Abbie had been speaking of was
herself. She had so wanted to believe that Dylan had
plans to ask her to marry him. But Abbie had pains-
takingly drawn a perfect cap of yellow hair on the
figure there on the bulletin board. Abbie had used a
yellow crayon to carefully etch short, straight, chin-
length tresses—so different from her own shoulder-
length, curly, auburn hair.

T.C. was Abbie's mother.

The childish picture explained everything. Yet, it
explained nothing. She needed to talk to Dylan. She
needed to talk to T.C.

As if Laura had conjured her image with that
thought, T.C. slipped into the room. She looked pale,
her eyes red-rimmed.

"I guess you want to know who I really am."
T.C.'s features melted into a miserable countenance,
and fresh tears threatened to spill.

"I kind of figured that out," Laura said. Even
though T.C. had a lot of explaining to do, Laura's
heart ached with compassion for this young woman.
"We do need to discuss what's going on, but not
right now. Right now you have a job to do." She
glanced at the paint-speckled children. "Are you up
to it?"

T.C. nodded.

"I'm going to get myself cleaned up, and then I'm
going to talk to Dylan."

At the mention of Dylan's name, fear lit T.C.'s
blue eyes. "Before you do, Laura, please let me explain—"

Laura stopped her with an upraised palm. "Not
now," she said. "You take care of these children.
I'll give you all the time you need this afternoon,
after the children leave for the day. They've been
upset enough and they need your undivided attention."

T.C. nodded resignedly. "I understand," she said,
her voice barely a whisper. "I'll be waiting for you
when you get back."

The elevator doors closed, boxing Laura into the
tight, lonely space with a multitude of enormous,
overwhelming thoughts running through her mind.

How could this have happened? How could she

have hired T.C.—Abbie's mother—to work at the
Mitchell Corporation day care without realizing who
the woman was? But, then again, how could she have
known? Dylan had never talked about his ex-wife.

Laura pictured Dylan's angry face as he'd shouted
at her. *What were you thinking to do this?* He'd
hurled the question at her.

Dear God! Dylan believed that she *knew* T.C. was
Abbie's mother. What thoughts must be running
through his head right now? He must be thinking that
she'd schemed and plotted with T.C. He must be
feeling so betrayed.

Compassion for him rose up in her, fierce and
strong. She felt guilty that her actions—no matter
that she was ignorant of T.C.'s true identity—had
caused Dylan one moment of grief.

But the guilt quickly became tinged around the
edges with irritation. Why would he think she'd do
such a thing to him? Why hadn't he stopped long
enough to realize that she'd never purposely hurt him
in any way?

Why hadn't he asked her to explain instead of as-
suming he knew all the answers? Her irritation flared
into full-fledged anger and insult.

"Stop." She spoke the word aloud, a resolute echo
bouncing off the shiny, confining walls of the elevator.

She couldn't let her emotions get the best of her—
not when she knew so little of the story. She had no
information regarding Dylan and T.C.'s past. She re-

fused to allow herself to make snap judgments, or any judgments for that matter, until she talked this over with Dylan.

The glowing numbers above the door slowly changed, then the elevator came to a halt. Laura hurried down the hallway toward Dylan's office.

His secretary looked ready for her.

"He said to tell you he's busy," the woman stated.

Laura brushed passed her. "He'll see me."

"But—"

Grasping the doorknob firmly, Laura opened the door and pushed her way inside.

Dylan stood across the room, looking out the window. He turned to glare at her. "I'm busy," he said, his tone flat and emotionless. Then he turned back toward the window.

"I can see that." She snapped the words at him and flung the door closed behind her. She'd promised herself not to let her emotions rule her, but his bald-faced lie was like a slap in the face.

"Where's Abbie?" she asked.

"Home. With Mrs. Nichols."

His big, broad back was like a wall between them as he continued to stare at the gray sky.

"Damn it, Dylan. You're going to talk to me. And you're going to talk to me now. You can't believe that I knew T.C. was your ex-wife." She fought the anger that simmered inside her at his silence. "She didn't use Mitchell as her last name. How was I to know? I tried to ask you about Abbie's mother, but you refused to talk about it. I didn't press—'' she stopped, knowing her words were running on top of one another, but feeling a sudden desperate need for him to believe she was innocent in this ''—because you made it seem as though it was a bad memory. I didn't want to pry—''

"It is a bad memory."

His voice sounded vapid, almost tedious, but Laura clearly heard the deep emotion steeping just below the surface.

"A *very* bad memory."

She pressed her lips together, hoping her silence would impel him to speak.

He turned to face her, his arms folded tight across his chest. "And *T.C.*, as you call her, didn't use the name Mitchell because we were never married."

A frown of confusion bit deeply into her brow. She waited for Dylan to elaborate, but the seconds ticked by and the silence grew longer and thicker and more tense.

Finally, she broke down and pleaded, "Talk to me, Dylan. Please."

His sigh was almost weary as he rubbed his hand across his forehead. When he looked at her, his dark gaze held something in it that Laura had never seen. An almost tangible vulnerability that cried out to her to have patience with him.

She lowered herself into one of the twin, high-backed wing chairs that faced his desk, hoping that if he saw she was relaxed then maybe he could be the same.

He sighed again, took a seat at his desk, rested his elbows on the desk top and curled his hands into a tight fist.

"This is hard," he said. "I'd rather not have to reveal any of this sordid tale to you. I'd rather you went on seeing me as you always have—confident...capable...caring...."

He let the sentence trail and Laura felt impelled to say, "But I do. And I will."

He gazed off over her left shoulder. His throat convulsed in a difficult swallow and she began to realize just how hard this discussion was for him.

"Well," he finally said, his words coming slowly, "Teresa Catherine Duffy reduced me to a pile of quivering, quaking..." The words died in his throat.

Teresa Catherine. Laura silently repeated the name in her head. *T.C.* The young woman had changed what she called herself in an effort to fool everyone, or at least Dylan.

But it was the description Dylan had given of himself—so different from the bold, virile man she'd come to know—that shocked and confused her to the point that she didn't know how to respond. So she didn't.

"Teresa decided that she was going hunting for a rich man," he continued. "She spent a small fortune on her trap, too—a fashion make-over that gave her a classy, professional air, expensive, upswept hairdos and just enough makeup to fool me into thinking she was a full-grown woman.'' He nodded slowly, his eyes glazing with the rancorous memory. "Yes, Teresa went hunting. And she snared me.''

He inhaled deeply. "I didn't have a chance. I was lost from the first moment I laid eyes on her. She was beautiful...vivacious. And oh, so sincere. I fell for it all because I wanted to believe that a beautiful young woman could fall for me.'' His sudden bark of laughter was sharp, bitter. "Can you imagine that? Me, a worldly-wise businessman, unable to hold my own against a nineteen-year-old fortune hunter?'' Again, his laugh was harsh. "But she was taught by the best, I can tell you that.''

Laura wondered what Dylan meant by T.C. "being taught by the best,'' but before she could ask he continued with his story.

"Teresa Duffy is the vilest of female creatures— she's a liar, a thief and a manipulator. She can conjure tears from thin air. She can connive—''

"Wait a minute,'' Laura said. This simply didn't sound like the T.C. who worked in her day care, the T.C. she'd spent hours, days and weeks with. "I'm sorry, but it's so hard for me to believe that you're talking about T.C. She doesn't look a day over twenty. How could you think she was...'' Words failed her. "She tried to manipulate you into marrying her?'' Laura knew she was unable to keep the dubiousness from her tone.

"Oh, she didn't have marriage on her mind." Dylan's words grated with anger. "No, she—"

"Wait. Wait just a minute," Laura said, waving her hand and shaking her head. "You're losing me. You said that T.C. was hunting for a rich man. But I need to back up a step, because I still can't understand how you thought she was—" she hesitated, unsure of how to go about saying what needed to be said "—old enough for you."

Dylan leaned back and pulled open his top desk drawer. After a moment of rummaging, he slammed the drawer closed and tossed a color picture on the desk top. It skidded to a stop a few inches from Laura at the edge of the desk. She reached over and straightened it.

The candid shot had been taken at a private party. Laura identified a smiling Dylan immediately. But she could hardly believe the sophisticated, coiffured woman at his side was T.C. Laura picked up the picture and, squinting, studied it. After a moment, she realized that the woman in the picture was, indeed, T.C.

"Dylan," she said, the breathy quality of her voice evincing her astonishment, "I can't believe this." Then her gaze once more found his. "But, if she wasn't looking for marriage...what was her motive?"

"Money."

His black eyes were hard and cold, and the dark

resentment brewing in them rendered Laura speechless.

"Our relationship moved along quickly," he said. "So quickly that I didn't have time to even begin to think that Teresa might have ulterior motives." A disgusted sound came from deep in his throat. "I didn't have time to think, period. Things between us turned…physical almost immediately. I couldn't believe that this woman—or what I thought was a woman—wanted me. I was flattered.… I was…I was…"

"Horny?" Laura offered. She didn't mean to harass him, but the word just seemed to fit like a well-placed puzzle piece.

He covered his face with his hands and ended up massaging his temples with his fingertips. Then, he looked at her. "Yeah," he said. "I guess that just about sums it up."

He inhaled deeply as though to steel himself for the rest of his story.

"Teresa told me she was protected. And like a fool, I believed every word she said. She became pregnant. And her attitude toward me changed in an instant."

Maybe it was because she was so naive, but for the life of her, Laura still couldn't seem to figure out T.C.'s scheme.

Dylan's tone turned somber as he revealed, "She planned on selling me the baby."

"What?" Laura felt she couldn't have possibly

heard him correctly. When he didn't answer her immediately, she helplessly repeated, "Sell you the baby?"

He nodded. Then every muscle in his body seemed to tense and there was raw pain in his eyes. "She threatened to have an abortion."

The memory alone was obviously agony for him. He chewed his bottom lip in an effort to control his emotions, his eyes glistening with unshed tears.

"It was the worst month of my life."

The starkness in his words made her believe him, and Laura's heart wrenched.

"Teresa played me like a tune," he said. "She pushed and pushed. Manipulating and finagling this "deal" she said we had to make. One day she bullied and threatened, the next she cried." He rubbed his hand across his chin. "All I knew for certain was that I didn't want my baby to die in some abortion clinic. Thank God, she finally agreed to a price." His gaze took on a pleading look. "Don't get me wrong, Laura. I'm all for women's rights. But that was *my* baby. *My* flesh and blood. *My* child that Teresa was threatening to abort. For no reason at all, other than extortion."

Fire lit in his eyes. "That baby meant nothing to her. Nothing! Abbie was just a pawn in some ugly game she was playing."

The anger in his voice was laced with something else, and the same instant she mentally identified it,

Laura found herself saying it. "You're embarrassed."

"You're damned right I'm embarrassed." His eyes were intense. "I'm a grown man. And I let myself get involved with some common, sordid little thief who took me for everything she could get." He sighed. "And now she's back."

"We'll deal with this, Dylan," Laura felt impelled to assure him.

"You're damned right about that, too," his voice boomed again and he slapped his hand on the desk, making her jump. "You're going to fire her, Laura! I don't want her within a hundred miles of Abbie, or me, or Mitchell Corporation. You're going to fire her. And you're going to do it today."

Chapter Six

Laura stood in the doorway and studied T.C. The young woman, unaware that she was being watched, worried a damp napkin between her fingers until it was nearly rubbed to shreds.

Knowing that Brian waited safe in the community playroom of the day care, building some imaginary castle kingdom, Laura focused all her attention on the problem at hand: T.C.'s deception.

The dread inside Laura at the thought of what she must do weighed on her like a load of heavy bricks. T.C. had become more to her than an employee—she'd become a friend. But now Laura was left to wonder just how much of that friendship had been manipulated by T.C. Had T.C. purposefully and carefully developed this relationship so that she could be close to Abbie? Laura hoped it wasn't true, but couldn't tamp down the deep suspicion that Dylan's story instilled in her. And she had to admit that, right at this moment, she felt a little used and betrayed by T.C.—maybe not to the extent that Dylan must feel, but she felt deceived, nonetheless. Was T.C. really capable of the plotting and scheming that Dylan had accused her of?

The silent question seemed to draw the woman's attention and she glanced toward the door. Laura clearly read the dark apprehension in T.C.'s blue eyes and it tugged at her more forgiving emotions— but not strongly enough to allow her to go without answers to her burning questions.

She studied T.C., the silence between them thickening to nearly a tangible thing. This woman had hurt Dylan, humiliated him to the point that he was distrusting of *all* women.

The revelation that T.C. was the cause of Dylan's wariness toward women struck like a physical blow. It propelled Laura's mind back all those many weeks ago to the night he had arrived in his sleek, black sports car and viciously accused her of taking advantage of his father, of having coerced money from the sickly gentleman. Unwittingly, Laura placed her fingers over her mouth. She understood his motives now. Better than she ever had before.

The urge to run back to his office, to comfort him, to reassure him that she wasn't anything like T.C. welled up inside her, hot and strong. But she couldn't do that right now, no matter how badly she might want to. Not with the need for some kind of explanation from T.C. burning inside her like a raging bonfire.

Finally, she spoke. "Tell me what you were thinking when you were trying to become pregnant with Abbie." Miraculously, Laura kept her tone steady, but she didn't even try to temper the accusation in her words.

"Laura, I *know* what I did was horrible." Tears welled in T.C.'s guilt-ridden gaze. She pressed her lips together for a moment to still their trembling. Then she stated, "I need you to understand that I'm trying to make up for my past."

Standing there, stiff and unyielding, Laura worked hard to keep her empathy at bay. She worked hard to encase her heart in some sort of armor plating against T.C.

"Please, Laura." A tear broke free and traveled slowly down T.C.'s cheek. "Don't judge me until we've had a chance to talk. Until I've had a chance to make you understand."

That one tiny teardrop should have been a weak and useless assault on the sheathing around Laura's tender emotions. But as water will do, it trickled into the cracks, seeped through the seams of her armor. Its heat melted all the cold, hard barriers with which it came into contact.

For a split second, Laura wavered. She wanted to believe T.C.'s anguish was sincere, but how could she know that the woman wasn't acting? How could she possibly know if T.C. was being honest? She wanted to believe everything that Dylan had said— every accusation against T.C. that he'd made. Yet, at the same time, she yearned for proof that she'd judged T.C.'s character correctly a few weeks ago when she'd hired her.

"How can I be sure that what you're telling me is the truth?" Laura asked.

"Oh, Laura." Another tear gathered on the outer rim of T.C.'s eye, so fat and heavy that it fell from her cheekbone onto her blouse, staining the cotton with a dark circle. "You have to believe me! I wouldn't lie. I'm through with lies and deceit—"

"How can you say that?" Laura asked, stepping into the room. "You got this job based on a lie. Everything you told me was a lie. I can't allow you to go on working in the day care when—"

"Please, Laura. *Please.* I'm begging you to sit down and listen." Her chin quivered and she dabbed at her nose with the limp, torn napkin. Her blue-eyed gaze locked onto Laura. "I'll tell you everything. I'll make you understand. Every terrible, true word of it."

There was something in those eyes. Something that banged, chinked and finally ripped away the metallic shell that surrounded Laura's heart.

Slowly she moved to the table, pulled out a chair and sat. "Okay, T.C.," she said, her voice barely a whisper. "Make me understand."

For nearly forty-five minutes, T.C. talked. And

even all these minutes later, Laura still could hardly begin to imagine the childhood T.C. had lived through, with an alcoholic, drug-abusing mother who was fixated on the idea of getting through life riding the coattails of wealthy men.

T.C.'s mother—if the woman could be called a mother—had borne two children by two different men, marrying neither of them. She'd moved in and out, traveled from man to man, sometimes being thrown out, but more often leaving a relationship that had become abusive, always looking for that elusive "rich one" who would take care of her forever. But men of the professional and financial caliber she searched for rarely, if ever, frequented the bars that were her hangouts. When the woman finally figured this out, she realized she could no longer rely on a face and body that had been ravaged by her hard lifestyle to get her what she wanted. That's when Juanita Duffy had turned to her daughter, and T.C.'s lessons began.

She was taught the fine art of flirting—relaying silent, sensuous messages with the body and eyes. She learned to dress provocatively, yet with enough class that her lowly upbringing wouldn't show through. Making the most of the outside trappings, Juanita buffed to a high gloss the gold that overlaid T.C.'s cheap, trashy background.

Those were the exact words T.C. had used, and Laura wondered—marveled even—that someone could think of herself in those self-deprecating terms.

T.C. must have had a terrible self-image, an extremely low self-esteem, both of which had been fostered by Juanita Duffy.

"Dylan didn't have a chance," T.C. murmured.

Laura remembered Dylan saying those very same words.

"Between me and Mama." T.C. shook her head, her blond, bobbed hair swinging gently.

"How on earth did you meet him?" Laura could hold back her questions no longer.

"It wasn't easy." The memory brought a chuckle that was purely reflex. "I spent lots of time at *the* socially correct nightclub, with no luck. Then I found the boat marina down on the Chesapeake Bay." She shook her head again. "Nothing. And I was actually physically removed from the country club here in the city." Her blue eyes lit humorously as she quipped, "You must be a member, you know." Pushing her hair back from her face, she sobered. "I know it isn't funny. But I have to laugh or I'd cry."

She sighed wearily. "Mama read a story in the paper about Dylan. He'd designed some kind of computer software or something. They took a picture of him and that shiny black sports car he owns. It was easy finding Mitchell Corporation and watching for him." She shrugged. "It was even easier to step out in front of his car."

"You what?"

"Well, actually Mama sort of gave me a little push. But it was a brilliant plan."

What kind of crazy woman was this Juanita Duffy?
Laura wondered, to push her daughter out in front of
a moving automobile.

"Oh, I didn't get hurt," T.C. said. "Only shook
up a little. But I played it up real good. Dylan took
me inside his big fancy office. Had his secretary fix
me a cup of tea in a dainty little china cup." Her
tone softened. "He treated me really nice from the
very beginning."

"And you took advantage of his kindness." The
words left her mouth before she'd realized it, but she
wouldn't have silenced the truth even if she could
have.

T.C. swallowed and looked her directly in the eye.
"Yes, I did," she admitted calmly. "But you have
to remember that I really and truly thought I was
doing the right thing."

Laura felt her face screwing up with astonishment.
"The right thing?"

"To *survive*," T.C. stressed, then her words came
faster, closer together as she continued. "After he'd
slept with me once, I knew I couldn't marry him. He
was just so…nice. I couldn't let Mama get her hooks
into him. She'd never have let him go. But Mama
kept pushing and pushing. And my heart was beginning to tell me that this was wrong. I was so confused. There was so little money left. But how were
we going to *live*?" T.C. seemed to run out of steam
and she inhaled slowly and deeply.

"Anybody in your family ever hear of a job?" It

was a silly, rhetorical question, Laura knew, and she wasn't surprised when it went unanswered.

After a moment, T.C. went on with her story. "Then I found out I was pregnant. Mama was so happy. She was certain that Dylan Mitchell would make an honest woman of me. But by then I *knew* what I was doing was wrong."

The tissue she'd been holding was now a tight ball in her fist. She tossed it at the garbage can, but missed by a good foot.

"Mama was furious when I told her I wouldn't trap Dylan into marrying me. She told me if I wouldn't do things her way, then I could just fend for myself. Mama left, and I haven't seen her since. I have no idea where she is or what she's doing."

"Good riddance," Laura muttered. *You're better off without her,* she observed silently.

"I went to Dylan and confessed everything. It was all my fault, and I told him so." T.C. took a deep breath. "I told him I'd have an abortion. And he hit the roof. He wouldn't hear of it. He offered me money to have the baby. Enough money to get myself a good education." She licked her lips. "And I took it." Her inhalation was shaky. "At one point, early on, I told him I thought my...taking his money was wrong. I told him that I felt I really should have the abortion." Her voice became quiet. "He offered me even more money." She closed her eyes, as though she was trying to hide from this final confession. "And, God help me, but I told him I'd take it.

I told him I'd have the baby, give him custody. And that he'd never see me again."

Laura captured T.C.'s gaze. "What changed your plans?"

The young woman was silent a moment, and when she answered her tone was husky with deeply felt emotion. "I became a mother." Her blue eyes pleaded for understanding. "Laura, I made those promises before I had Abbie, before I held her, before I looked into that precious face of hers."

Tears welled in T.C.'s eyes, spilling unheeded down her cheeks, and Laura felt a painful wrenching in her heart.

"Laura, I *hated* to leave my daughter. I didn't want to. But I *had* to." T.C. leaned her weight forward. "I had to get my life straightened out. I wanted to get myself an education. I needed to...adjust my...attitude...and my priorities. My head was so messed up. I didn't want to be like Mama." She pulled another tissue from the box and dabbed her nose. "I wanted to become a mother that Abbie could be proud of. Besides...how could I ever explain to my daughter that I was willing to give her up...for money?" T.C.'s eyes closed and she sobbed, her shoulders shaking as years of carefully controlled emotion rolled over her like a wildly careering freight train.

Watching her friend finally surrender to the sadness and guilt that plagued her, Laura felt an urgent need to reach out and comfort her. T.C.'s fist was clenched tight when she slid her palm over top of it. Laura sat there, silent, and allowed T.C. to expend her pent-up tears.

Some minutes later T.C. began to get herself under control. She wiped the dampness from her cheeks and inhaled shakily. "Laura, I know you have to fire me, and I'll go, because I don't want to get you into trouble with Dylan." Her voice was as trembly as her inhalation. "I can find another job. But do you think there's any way that you can maybe let me know how Abbie's doing?"

Closing her eyes against the empathy that prickled behind her lids, Laura barely restrained herself from crying. She drew in a long breath through her nose, trying hard to keep the tears at bay. She raised her gaze to T.C.'s and swallowed with difficulty around the lump that had formed in her throat.

Laura wanted to say something that would make this whole bad situation go away. God, how she wanted to find some words that would make everything right. But she couldn't get the air past her larynx, couldn't get her tongue to form even one syllable.

"I'm sorry," T.C. said, her eyes filling with fresh tears. "I know I'm asking too much." She shook her head. "But she's my daughter, Laura. Abbie's my baby! It's going to kill me to just walk away from her."

Something in Laura snapped. She had to do something to help T.C. Sitting by and doing nothing when someone was in trouble or pain was not in her makeup, it wasn't who she was.

Yes, T.C. had done something dishonorable—something immoral, in fact. But the woman had had some bad influences in the past. And she was trying to straighten out her life. She was trying to turn things around. Trying to right a wrong.

Again, Laura swallowed around the emotion lodged in her throat. "T.C.," she began haltingly, "we'll work this out. You can keep your job here at the day-care center. I'll talk to Dylan. I'll make him understand that you need to see Abbie."

"Oh, Laura." T.C. reached out and grasped Laura's forearm in a viselike grip. "Thank you! Thank you *so* much. I can't tell you what this means to me."

The deep, sincere appreciation that gushed from T.C.'s voice, her eyes, her very posture touched Laura to the core.

"I'll talk to Dylan," Laura repeated her promise. "I'll fix this."

The hope and gratitude T.C. felt was obviously too much for her to handle, and once again the woman began to cry softly. And as Laura sat there, the vow she'd just made weighed like a cape of lead on her shoulders. How on earth could she fix this? How could she possibly help T.C. when she remembered Dylan's bitterness and anger with such vivid clarity?

"I heard some of the kids talking this afternoon." Brian sat in the bucket seat of the car and snapped his seat belt around his waist. "They said Abbie won't be coming to the day care anymore."

Laura felt the need to be honest with her son as she inserted the key in the ignition and revved the engine. "Well, honey," she said, "that's what Dylan said today. But I'm going to talk to him. I'm going to try and change his mind."

"Is it true that T.C. is Abbie's mom?"

"Um-hmm," she answered. "It is."

"Good." Brian nodded his approval. "Cause Abbie really needs a mom. She's really been talkin' a lot about wantin' her mom lately."

"Yes, she has," Laura agreed softly. *And I thought she'd been wanting me. That Dylan had been planning to...* She let the painful thought trail off.

Brian's gaze was wide-eyed and innocent as he said, "Everybody needs their mom. I don't know what I'd do without you."

She smiled lovingly at her son, her whole body tingling with maternal warmth. "Thanks, pal. I don't know what I'd do without you, either."

Her son's comment may have been entirely innocent, but at the same time it was utterly true.

Everybody needs their mom.

The words echoed in her head. She had to find the right words to persuade Dylan that Abbie needed to know T.C. Laura sat a little straighter in the seat, tilted her chin up a fraction, as she was filled with a strong conviction.

"Thanks, Brian," she said.

"For what?"

She shrugged. "I'm going to talk to Dylan about Abbie coming back to the day care and spending some time with T.C. I was worried about what I was going to say." She chuckled. "I still don't know what I'm going to say, but I *do* agree with you that Abbie needs her mom."

Brian became very still. "Maybe I should go with you."

Laura's brow creased. "To talk to Dylan?" she asked.

"Yeah."

She patted him on the knee. "I appreciate the thought. But I think I ought to do this on my own." She took her eyes off the road for a moment to study him. "If you don't mind my asking, though, why did you offer?"

"'Cause I heard Dylan shouting this afternoon," he admitted. "Then I heard everybody saying Abbie wouldn't be back. If you're going to try and change his mind, you're going to have trouble." Then he shook his head, breathlessly adding, "T-r-u-b-e-l."

Laura felt a dark, ominous cloud descend upon her. Her son might need a little help with his spelling, but he'd assessed the situation perfectly.

The heavy, oppressive apprehension that had settled on her during the drive home remained with her throughout the evening. She fixed Brian's dinner and put a load of laundry into the washer. After the living-room tables had been dusted, she ran the vacuum, even though she'd just cleaned the carpet the night before last. She knew very well that she was avoiding what was waiting for her—that inevitable confrontation with Dylan.

Right about seven-thirty, the sky began to glow with a rosy hue of an early autumnal sundown. She was standing at the window, staring with unseeing eyes at the trees in the side yard. Her stomach churned and she could hardly breathe from the weight of the dread that pressed against her chest.

She wasn't going to fire T.C. Her sense of justice simply wouldn't allow her to do it. But how on earth was she going to tell Dylan? How could she possibly make him realize that she was only trying to do the right thing?

Closing her eyes, she exhaled soulfully. She couldn't make him understand. She knew that. No amount of explanation on her part would make him accept her motives. No amount of talking would make him comprehend that Abbie needed—no, Laura silently amended, Abbie had a *right* to know her own mother.

Dylan's animosity was based on the fact that he had been tricked by T.C. His anger had deep-seated roots that fed on some extremely dark emotions: humiliation and embarrassment. These feelings were frozen somewhere inside him, somewhere beneath rational thought, so that even if she did make a logical argument for T.C., Dylan's subconscious would never let him understand.

But she had to try. She had to at least tell him her decision to keep T.C. on at the day care, and try to persuade him to allow Abbie...

Through the low-lying bushes, Laura saw the bright lights of the garage flicker on. And even though the building was at least a hundred yards from the window, she could hear the angry clatter of tools and she instinctively knew Dylan was the person in the garage.

She checked on Brian and told him she was going out to the garage to speak with Dylan. Her son looked up from the huge contraption he was building with his erector set and nodded, worry creasing his brow. Laura assured him everything would be okay.

But as she walked across the yard, the dread she felt nearly overwhelmed her. Even though she realized that justness and virtue were on her side, she had to admit that she now knew how the legendary David felt when he went out alone on the battlefield to face the giant Goliath.

Chapter Seven

As she reached the door of the garage, Laura could hear Dylan mumbling, but couldn't yet see him because he was in front of his car with the hood up.

"Damn!"

She stopped short at the sound of his explosive expletive. A plastic bucket skittered across the cement floor and slid to a stop at her feet. Immediately, he came into view and saw her.

His stormy gaze studied her for an instant, then he bent down to the bucket. When his eyes raised to hers, some of the anger had left them, but not enough to ease the apprehension rolling inside her stomach.

"I'm sorry," he said. "I didn't know you were standing there."

She glanced pointedly at the bucket that lay at her feet and then back at Dylan.

"It was in my way," was all he said.

Laura remained silent and moved to the side of the car. Dylan went to the toolbox and rooted around intently.

"Abbie's angry with me," he stated without looking up. "I had Mrs. Nichols come and pick her up this afternoon after that…after that…fiasco at the day care."

He moved to the front of the car armed with a steel socket wrench. After positioning himself flat on his back on the wheeled creeper, he slid underneath the engine. The lower portion of his body was all that was visible to her—taut stomach, trim hips, and legs that were covered in soft, worn denim. Laura swallowed, took her top lip between her teeth and forced herself to glance away from the distracting sight.

"When I got home, Abbie refused to let me in her room," he said. "Mrs. Nichols said Abbie cried for hours this afternoon. All she talked about was *her*. How I was keeping Abbie away from *her*. How she wanted to be with *her*."

The ugly emphasis Dylan placed on the feminine pronoun left Laura no doubt that he was speaking of T.C., and that he couldn't even bring himself to say her name.

"Damn," he whispered. "I can't see the bolt. Can you hand me the work light?"

Moving around to the front of the car, Laura took the light from the hook on the inside of the hood and crouched down beside him. He reached out for the light, his hand accidentally brushing her calf, and she felt a delicious rush of adrenaline flutter across her skin.

"Sorry," he murmured.

She handed him the light, but remained in her bent-kneed position by his side. Suddenly he slid out from under the car.

"Doesn't she realize that I'm only trying to protect her?" His dark eyes pleaded with her for understanding.

"She's so young, Dylan."

He searched her gaze for one silent, tension-filled instant, during which her heart nearly ripped in two. She *did* understand his fierce need to protect his daughter. Yet, at the same time, she understood T.C.'s need to know Abbie, too. Dear Lord, what was the answer to this horrible dilemma?

Dylan sighed, relaxed back onto the creeper and pushed himself back under the car.

He worked in silence a few moments, moments that Laura spent being mesmerized by the minute movements of his leg muscles. The worn material of his blue jeans was thin and molded to his rock-hard thighs. The long sinew of one thigh tensed, then relaxed as he maneuvered himself to just the right position in the tight confines.

Her mouth went dry as she remembered splaying her hand on his lower thigh the evening they had spent on the swing looking at the night sky. Absently, she ran her tongue over her cottony lips, and she inhaled shakily. She couldn't see how there would be any more nights like that one if she crossed him in this situation.

And she was certain that was how he would view her refusal to fire T.C.—as her crossing him. But she simply didn't see that she had any other choice. She had to do what was right for Abbie.

"Well," Dylan said, "Abbie will get over this. Once Teresa…T.C.—whatever the hell she's calling herself nowadays—once she's gone, this will all blow over. And things will get back to normal."

Tell him, she commanded herself. *Tell him you have no intention of firing T.C.* Laura closed her eyes tight, unable to bring herself to do what she knew had to be done.

"I'm not sure," she began slowly, "it's going to be that easy."

His legs went still, and instinctively she reached out and touched his knee in an effort to cushion the blow she was about to hurl at him.

"I'm not—" The words stuck in her throat. She steeled herself and started again. "I'm not going to fire T.C."

He shot from under the car and she snatched her hand tight against her.

"Like hell you're not."

The fury on his face, in his eyes, frightened her. *Stay calm,* she reminded herself. *You came in here knowing he was going to be upset with your decision.*

"You *are* going to fire her." He sat up, his face uncomfortably close to hers. "And if you don't, I will!"

"But...you can't do that."

"Watch me," he snapped.

She saw his lips thin with the rage he felt.

"That's what it means to be president of a company, Laura. I can do whatever I please. I have the right to protect my daughter!"

Something in Laura splintered. Her good intentions to remain calm somehow evaporated, and what took their place was a mixture of bewilderment and anger.

"But we had an agreement," she told him, trying hard to hold from her tone the betrayal she felt. "I'm in charge of the day care. I make the decisions—"

"Until I—" he poked himself in the chest "—as president of Mitchell Corporation, feel the decisions you make are wrong."

Laura felt her eyes narrow. "T.C. will remain an employee of the day care."

Dylan pushed himself to a stand, wiping his greasy hands down the thighs of his jeans as he moved.

"Then Abbie won't be coming to the day care!" he roared.

Laura stood, and watched him look up at the ceiling.

"What am I saying?" he asked no one in particular. His fiery gaze locked onto Laura. "The final decision is mine to make. And I will not issue a paycheck to Teresa Duffy. Not after the pain she put me through. Not after the misery she caused—''

''And that's just it, isn't it, Dylan?'' Every bit of emotion she felt was expressed in the question. ''*Your* pain. *Your* misery. You aren't going to forget it. You're going to make T.C. pay for the rest of her life.'' Her jaw was tight as she added, ''And Abbie will be paying right along with her.''

He looked at her hard. ''What do you mean by that? I'm trying to protect my daughter from a ruthless manipulator. Look how Teresa...or T.C—'' his rage exploded suddenly ''—whatever the hell the woman's name is! Look how she lied and manipulated to get the job at the day care to begin with.''

The silence throbbed with so much tense emotion that Laura found it hard to breathe.

''I will admit,'' she said, ''that T.C. wasn't entirely truthful—''

''Wasn't truthful? The woman changed her name! Don't let yourself be taken in by her, Laura. You're smarter than that.''

''All I know,'' she said, ''is that T.C. made some mistakes in the past. And we all make mistakes.'' This statement was terse and pointed. ''She confessed everything to me, Dylan. She feels the need to make things right.''

He made a disgusted sound in the back of his throat. ''And you believed her.''

''Yes,'' she said, ''I believed her. I still believe her. And I think you should talk to her.''

His eyes grew cold. "Like hell I will."

She tried to ignore the way his gaze froze her to her very soul. "I also think you should consider letting Abbie get to know her."

All he said was, "Never."

Laura could feel her frustration getting the best of her.

"T.C. has a right to know her daughter."

"T.C. gave up her rights years ago!" His tone turned vicious now.

The anger they had slung back and forth between them solidified into a thick, impenetrable wall. Laura hadn't meant the discussion to turn ugly like this, but the things he'd said had sent her over the edge of reason.

"I can't make you bring Abbie to the day care," she told him. "Even though it *is* the right thing to do. I can't force you to allow Abbie to see her mother." She pointed her index finger at him. "But I *can* keep you from firing T.C. I can. And I will. We had an agreement, you and I. A verbal contract. And you know it. You run Mitchell Corporation. I run the day care. And I say T.C. stays."

She turned and stalked to the door. When she reached it, she faced him once more. "Now, for the rest of it, I can only hope you'll listen to your conscience. You can wallow in your pain. You can dwell on the embarrassment that T.C. has caused you. Or..." She paused. "You can get over it."

One of his dark brows raised. "You make it sound so easy."

She glared at him. "You're only hurting yourself, you know." Then she amended, "That's not entirely true. You're hurting Abbie, too." *And T.C.,* she wanted to add, but thought better of it.

Cocking her head to one side, she asked, "Did you ever stop to realize that, if T.C. hadn't played that horrible game of manipulation, you wouldn't have that beautiful, blond-haired daughter of yours?" She raised her brows, but really didn't expect him to respond.

"And one more thing," she said. "You've spoken of your right to protect your daughter. And you've said in no uncertain terms how you believe T.C. has no rights here. But what about Abbie?" She let the question linger in the air. "Your daughter may only be four years old, but don't you think she has a right to know she has a mother who loves her?"

Her steady gaze was sharp and intense for one, drawn-out moment before she spun around on her heel and left him alone, desperately hoping he'd think long and hard about all that she'd said.

Dylan finished changing the oil in his car, all the while seething inside. How dare Laura betray him like this? It was bad enough that Teresa Duffy—T.C., he ruefully reminded himself—had slunk back into his life. It was bad enough that the woman had gotten a job with his company without his knowledge. *And* that she obviously had every intention of seeing Abbie behind his back. But to have Laura, his new business associate—*Come on now,* his subconscious silently needled, *she's become more to you than that.* But for her to side with T.C. against him was the ultimate breach of faith, the ultimate humiliation.

He washed his greasy hands, hoping the hot, soapy water that sluiced over his skin would cleanse away some of the bitter anger burning in his gut. But after turning off the spigot and towel-drying his hands, he realized that his anger only seemed to intensify with each passing second. Laura might as well rip his heart out of his chest and serve it on a silver platter.

He gritted his jaw tightly. He wouldn't let his emotions get the better of him. Hell, who was he kidding? His emotions had been ruling him all day long, and into the evening. His dented toolbox could attest to that. Laura's actions hurt him more than words could describe.

Turning off the overhead lights in the garage, he slipped out into the darkness toward his house, refusing even to look in the direction of the small cottage where she was staying.

How could she do this? How could she let herself be taken in by T.C.? The questions reverberated in his skull as he went inside and up the darkened stairway.

He felt as though the two of them had teamed up together to make his life a living hell. He stopped short, his foot poised on the top step. Could Laura have known T.C.'s real identity all along? Could she have helped to plan—

"No." He murmured the word aloud, shaking his head.

He'd only known Laura a short few weeks, but in that time he'd found out that she was like no other woman he'd ever met. She was no liar. She wasn't a schemer like T.C. Duffy.

Why then didn't Laura understand that it was imperative to protect Abbie from the likes of T.C.?

Drawn by the wedge of soft light coming from the narrow opening of Abbie's bedroom door, he peeked in. The door slid open with the barest touch. The low-wattage night-light lit the room in a golden glow. He moved to the bed and eased down to sit on the very edge of the mattress next to his sleeping daughter.

Abbie's shoulders rose and fell with the steady rhythm of sleep, and as Dylan watched her, he felt as though his heart could not possibly hold all the love he felt for this little cherub-faced imp. When her big, blue eyes gazed up at him lovingly, he knew he could conquer the world. There was nothing he wouldn't do for her.

"Mommy."

Somewhere between a sigh and a murmur, the word escaped his daughter's dream. Dylan felt his throat nearly swell shut. He turned his head, the satiny, golden light splintering into a thousand shards as he blinked back tears.

Was his darling little girl going to betray him, too?

He reached out and smoothed back her fine, silky-textured hair. Leaning forward, he intended to kiss her on the temple, but stopped and stared.

Her eyelashes were damp and clumped together. And her cheeks were stained with the tracks of dried tears. His baby girl was hurting.

Dylan felt an overwhelming desire to gather her up in his arms, cuddle her tight and whisper that everything was going to be okay. But he didn't. He couldn't bring himself to disturb her sleep just because he was the one who needed to be comforted.

You're hurting Abbie, too. Laura's words came back to haunt him in the darkness. *Abbie has rights.*

He gently ran his finger down Abbie's jaw and marveled at how velvety-soft her skin felt.

You can wallow in your pain...dwell on your embarrassment.

Was Laura right? Is that what he'd been doing all these years? he wondered.

Hell, no, came the silent answer. He'd only been protecting himself. And his little one, he thought as he tenderly touched the slight cleft in his daughter's chin.

Was that so wrong? The question caused his throat to once again knot with emotion.

You're hurting Abbie...you're hurting Abbie...

In protecting himself, had he unwittingly hurt his

daughter? He certainly never meant to. He'd never in his life want to cause her any kind of sorrow or pain. He loved her more than words could express.

Leaning forward, he rested his elbows on his knees and cradled his head in his hands. The weight of the world seemed to press in on him as he searched his soul for some kind of solution.

The security guard at Mitchell Corporation opened the door for Laura and Brian as they entered the building. Laura enjoyed bringing her son to work with her in the mornings. She had worked out a nice plan with the local school system in which the school buses picked up the elementary-aged children right at the front door of Mitchell Corporation. Likewise, in the afternoon the students were dropped off for after-school care. It was a perfect arrangement for the company employees and the children.

But today Laura felt a tremendous amount of guilt over the fact that she'd forgotten that tomorrow was Brian's birthday and she'd promised to bake cookies for him to take to school to share with his classmates. This business between Dylan, Abbie and T.C. had scattered her thoughts like multihued leaves on the brisk autumn wind.

This day-care center had been her biggest dream, but when she remembered the quiet, stable life she and Brian had lived before moving to Wilmington, she was left wondering if her success might have cost her something dear, something irreplaceable.

"This evening on the way home, we'll stop at the store and pick up all the ingredients we need to make peanut-butter cookies," she promised him.

"Can I lick the spoon?" he asked with a big grin.

"You sure can."

"Thanks, Mom."

Brian reached out and slipped his hand into hers. The action took her by surprise and she squeezed his fingers, silently vowing that she wouldn't let this ordeal with Dylan take precedence over her responsibilities as a parent.

She knew Dylan felt he was trying to be the best father he could be for Abbie; she might not agree with his opinions or his actions, but she could relate to his motives. And she wanted to set her priorities straight, as well.

When she saw the lights were on in the day care, she frowned. Usually the first to arrive, she made a practice of turning on the lights and getting things set up each day. It was a job she enjoyed, a job she looked forward to.

Her spine stiffened when she looked through the heavy glass front door and saw Dylan standing in the community play area. Seeing how his shoulders were squared, his arms folded across his chest, Laura could tell he was ready for a confrontation. Her stomach tightened with dark anxiety. She didn't need another argument with him, not now.

Steeling herself against his anger, she pushed her way inside.

"I don't want to fight, Dylan," was her greeting. "Not in front of Brian."

His gaze was cold as obsidian.

"Laura! Brian!" Abbie's high-pitched voice called their attention from across the room.

Laura felt her dangling earrings swing, so quickly did she turn her head and look at Dylan's daughter.

"Hi, Abbie," Brian said.

"I get to see my mommy today." The smile on Abbie's face was bright as a ray of sunshine.

Laura had to make a conscious effort to keep her jaw from actually dropping open. Her brow creased with bewilderment as she focused her querying eyes on Dylan. *What's going on?* her gaze silently asked. But all she got from him was that black, stony stare.

"Brian, you still have twenty minutes before the other children are due in and the bus comes," she said without taking her eyes from Dylan's face. "Would you mind sitting out here with Abbie while her father and I go into my office to talk?"

"Sure, Mom." Brian pulled his backpack from his shoulders and set it on the table before crossing the room to Abbie.

Her tone grew quiet when she next addressed Dylan. "Would you mind stepping into my office, so we can talk? Or do you intend to keep your intentions all to yourself?"

His chin tipped up in an almost arrogant fashion. "Oh, believe me, I intend to make things unbelievably clear. To you, *and* to T.C."

Without another word, Laura walked down the hallway and knew, from the sound of his footfalls, that Dylan followed her. She entered the room, flipped on the overhead light and placed her purse on the desk. He began talking at her before she even had a chance to turn around.

"I'm not certain that having Abbie come here is the right thing," he began. "And I will admit that I'm scared out of my wits that it's absolutely *wrong* for her."

"It's not, Dylan, believe me—"

His cold glare cut her off. And if it hadn't, the anger she read in his tense jaw would have.

He blames me for all this. The thought smacked her so unexpectedly that she was overtaken by a strong sense of guilt before she could even think. *Had* she forced Dylan into doing something he really didn't want to do? Had the things she'd said to him last night coerced him into bringing Abbie here to spend time with T.C. when he seriously felt it was wrong for his daughter? The questions bombarded her and had her second-guessing herself.

Should she have kept her nose out of the situation entirely? Should she have just fired T.C. as Dylan had first requested? If she had, her life would be so much simpler now. If she had, she wouldn't have built this wall between herself and this wonderful man whom she had come to love so much.

Laura inhaled sharply. Where on earth had that idea come from?

All the doubting questions, added to this shocking revelation that she loved Dylan, started her thoughts spinning and spinning, until her mind was overflowing with guilt, anxiety and uncertainty—and some joyous emotion she couldn't put a name to.

"Can we talk?" Her query sounded weak and shaky to her ears.

"I don't care to talk about this," he stated. "All I do want to do is tell you what I expect from you."

She bristled at the harsh tone of his voice. *He does blame me,* she realized. Silently, she searched his gaze. And the severe glint in his jet-black eyes left her feeling empty and deprived.

"T.C. will not be left alone with my daughter." The statement was flat, nearly toneless. "I want another adult present at all times. Preferably you."

Laura shook her head slowly. "But that's impossible. T.C. alone is in charge of the four-year-old group. I'm needed to relieve each adult for a fifteen-minute break...or fill in if someone calls in sick."

"Then you'd better hire another employee." His tone brooked no argument. "Someone who will stick to T.C. like feathers on a bird."

Inhaling slowly, Laura fought back the irritation that was sparked by his words. This was his daughter they were talking about, she reminded herself. He had every right to make any kind of rule he wanted.

"Okay." The word came out in a near whisper.

"And T.C. is not to leave the premises with Abbie," he continued. "Under no circumstances is she to take my daughter outside of this building."

She nodded, then remembering the daily routine of the day care, she asked, "Can they go to the outside play area with the class?"

"With adult supervision."

Again, Laura nodded.

They stood within a couple of feet of each other, but they might as well have been miles apart, so cold and empty was the space between them, Laura experiencing a mind-numbing void and Dylan obviously feeling forced to do this thing against his will.

Silently, he turned to leave. He opened the door and fixed his eyes on her. She knew what he was going to say before he even opened his mouth. Unable to look at him, she focused her gaze at the spot where his hand clenched the doorknob.

"And one more thing," he said.

Laura's gut wrenched tight with a dark, nervous apprehension.

"If anything should go wrong—" his voice evinced every ounce of the pent-up emotion churning inside him "—I'll hold you personally responsible."

He walked out then, leaving her all alone behind her closed office door.

Chapter Eight

"Oh, Laura, it's just so...wonderful."

T.C.'s tone held a euphoric mixture of awe and disbelief, and she'd repeated that same statement at least a dozen times as Laura explained and stressed Dylan's strict rules regarding Abbie.

"It is wonderful," she agreed. "But do you understand that I need to sit in on your class until we can hire an aid? And that you'll have to give the others their breaks? Because Dylan refuses to allow—"

"I understand everything, Laura," T.C. said. "I really do. And it's fine with me." Her happiness bubbled over with light, tinkling laughter. "It's just so...wonderful. I'll be spending time with Abbie."

"But you still have a job to do," Laura told her. "You still have to care for the other children."

"Oh, I do understand. I really do."

So, for the rest of that week, Laura remained with
T.C. anytime Abbie was in the day-care center. Rou-
tinely, Dylan would bring his daughter in early, before T.C. arrived, and either he or Mrs. Nichols
would pick up Abbie in the afternoon.

Both Abbie and T.C. couldn't have been happier
with the arrangement. And, of course, Dylan was like
a bear with a festering paw. The fact that Abbie was
spending her days with her mother seemed to stick
under his skin like a jagged thorn. And he took every
bit of his surliness out on Laura.

No, his behavior might not be logical, Laura realized, but it was natural, understandable. Because
where T.C. and Abbie were concerned, Dylan didn't
deal in the rational—he simply surrendered to his
emotions. And all his emotions regarding T.C. were
negative and suspicious.

Although Laura understood all this, it was still
hard for her; it was hard not to feel guilty since she
knew Dylan blamed her for this whole situation, and
it was hard not to feel resentful toward him because
he faulted her when she'd only done what she'd
thought was best for Abbie.

By early the next week, Laura had hired an aid to
help T.C. with the four-year-olds. Amy was young,
just out of high school the year before. And in order
to help T.C. save face with her new assistant, Laura
decided not to divulge the sordid past and simply—

and firmly—suggested that Amy stick close to T.C. in order to learn every aspect of her job. T.C. understood the situation and was grateful for Laura's tact.

But even though she'd hired Amy, and even though she trusted T.C. implicitly, Laura still felt a tremendous responsibility where Abbie was concerned, and she found herself checking in on the four-year-old group off and on all during the day.

And as she sat at her desk, almost two weeks after hiring Amy, Laura felt a strong urge to look in on T.C.

The room was busy. Paper and crayons cluttered the large activity table as several children drew pictures. Amy was kept fully occupied as she helped one little boy trace a yellow circle that was obviously a big, bright sun over a square house. Laura spied another group of children in the dress-up area. Today T.C. had set up a supermarket and was acting as the cashier. One youngster who sported an old felt fedora pulled out a battered brown wallet and pretended to pay T.C. with play money.

"Thank you, sir," T.C. said as she took the money, made the cash register ding and then handed the boy some change. "Come again."

The boy nodded in a manly manner and tucked the bulky wallet into his pocket. Laura grinned when she watched him reach out, offer T.C. his hand and share a vigorous handshake.

Suddenly, Abbie caught her eye, the little girl tottering on shiny, high-heeled shoes, a feathered hat propped jauntily atop her silky blond hair. The child flung the fluffy pink boa over her shoulder and placed her purchases on the make-believe checkout counter. Laura actually had to press her fingertips to her lips to keep her mirth from escaping.

"How are you today, miss?" T.C. asked in a pleasant tone.

"I'm wonderful, daaaling."

Abbie's "adult" voice was so cute that Laura simply had to chuckle.

All eyes turned toward the door where Laura stood.

"Hi, Laura," T.C. called. "Come on in."

Just then Abbie staggered in the too-big shoes. She fell to the carpeted floor, scraping her knee on the corner of the table leg.

T.C. was around the table and at her daughter's side in an instant. Laura saw blood welling up on Abbie's skin, and when she heard the little girl begin to cry she felt a rush of sympathy sweep through her.

"It looks like you need a little bandage on that knee, Abbie," Laura said, kneeling down.

Abbie sniffed and nodded her agreement.

"But don't put no stinging medicine on it," the little boy in the felt fedora stated.

"We won't do that, Joey," Laura assured him. "Abbie, why don't you come with me and—"

"I want my mommy to do it!"

Fresh tears sprang to Abbie's eyes.

"Okay." Laura's tone was soft and soothing. "T.C., take her to the…" The look on T.C.'s face made Laura hesitate.

"I…I can't, Laura," T.C. whispered.

Laura suddenly remembered Dylan's rule that Abbie not be left alone with her mother.

"Oh," she said. "Well, I'll go along. Amy, can you manage a few minutes on your own?"

"Sure," Amy said from across the room.

"We won't be long," Laura said as she and T.C. headed out the door with Abbie in tow.

The counter in the powder room was large enough so that T.C. could sit Abbie on it and have a closer look at the child's injury.

"It's not too bad," T.C. crooned lovingly. "Let's wash it with a little soap and warm water and then I'll put a nice bandage on it."

Although she'd stopped crying, Abbie's lashes were still damp and her breathing was catchy with emotion. "Will it hurt?" she asked.

"I'll be as gentle as I can, sweetie," T.C. promised. "But we really need to clean it good before we cover it up. Isn't that right, Laura?"

"Um-hmm," Laura agreed. "If there are germs on your scrape, then you could get an infection."

"I'd better use some antiseptic, too," T.C. said.

Standing back near the supply cabinet, Laura

watched as mother ministered to daughter. It was so very obvious by the way T.C. tenderly cared for Abbie that this woman loved her little girl. Laura's heart squeezed with sentiment.

She hated to think that by enabling T.C. and Abbie to get together she had damaged her relationship with Dylan. But seeing these two together, Laura knew it was right, knew it was good. She tried to push aside the knowledge of what this situation had cost her, and concentrate on the warm pleasantness that washed through her at the sight of this little girl being cuddled by her loving mother.

Laura sensed a presence behind her and turned. There, in the open doorway, was Dylan, his gaze riveted to the maternal scene before him.

His handsome face was marred by the deep crease of concern that knit his brows together. The very sight of him started Laura's insides churning. The sheer strength of the attraction she felt for this man continued to startle her. She wanted to rush to him, to reassure him that he needn't worry about Abbie. But she knew how he felt, or thought she knew. He wouldn't appreciate any kind of comfort coming from her. The thought made her shoulders droop with despair. What had she done to their relationship?

"Daddy!" Abbie's face lit up when she noticed her father.

"What happened?" he asked, his tone as curt as it was gruff.

"She's okay," Laura hurried to assure him. His sharp, black eyes didn't even glance her way.

"I fell down," Abbie explained. "But Mommy fixed me right up."

"She really is okay, Dylan," T.C. said. But he ignored her also.

"I decided to take the rest of the day off," he told Abbie. "Get your things together and I'll take you to lunch. Then we'll go to the park or something."

Abbie squealed with delight. "Can Mommy come too?"

For a split second, the silence was so thick and tense Laura thought the very air had congealed. She watched as Dylan's jaw muscle clenched tight.

"Oh, honey," T.C. said to Abbie, "I couldn't possibly go. I have to work." She smoothed her palm along her daughter's cheek. "But you go with your dad and have a good time."

T.C. helped Abbie off the counter and the little girl rushed into her father's waiting arms. The two of them disappeared down the hall without another word.

Laura stood there in the powder room feeling so empty inside.

"It's so…hard." T.C. whispered the words almost to herself.

"For everyone," Laura said, unable to take her eyes off the vacant doorway.

* * *

The next afternoon, Laura walked down the hall toward Dylan's office, a mixture of emotions mingling in her chest. She'd received a call from his secretary that morning. Evidently Laura's signature was needed on some Mitchell Corporation documents.

She tried hard to fight the resentment she felt toward Dylan, understanding his treatment of her was caused by his emotional state of mind. But she'd be lying if she didn't admit to feeling irritated. She might understand how he felt, but damn it, he didn't have to take it out on her, did he?

Apparently, yes.

A deep sense of sadness rolled over her like a heavy, gray cloud. She missed Dylan—missed spending time with him, missed feeling all those intimate emotions he conjured in her. It was so sad to think that just when their relationship had started to bloom and grow, there had been this awful mess with T.C. and Abbie that choked off the attraction Laura and Dylan had felt for each other.

Well, she thought, that wasn't quite so. The attraction *she* felt for *him* hadn't diminished one iota. The idea that she'd done something to destroy the attraction Dylan had felt for her cause a mantle of melancholy to settle on her shoulders.

Maybe if she just talked to him about the situation, if she tried to explain…

She inhaled deeply. No, she thought. She already

had explained how she felt, and why she felt that way. That's what got her into this predicament to begin with.

Heaving another solemn sigh, Laura entered the open area where Dylan's secretary usually sat. The woman was away from her desk, but the door of his office was open and he looked up and motioned her inside.

"I'm buying the rights to a new software program," he said.

The way he got straight down to business only heightened the sense of sadness that weighed on her so heavily.

"I need your signature on these papers. You'll be stipulating how much of Mitchell Corporation you own and that you're aware of the purchase."

He paused for a split second, his piercing eyes studying her. "This is a good move for the company financially."

The prices he quoted for cost versus profit surprised Laura. He went on to explain a little about the uses of the software product to which they were buying the rights.

"So," he finally said, "does this sound okay with you?"

She nodded, trusting him totally where the business was concerned. She only wished she could trust him with her honest feelings and emotions where this situation with T.C. was concerned.

He pushed some legal documents across the desk. "Sign here," he instructed.

She picked up a pen and scrawled her name.

"And here." He turned the page and pointed at the blank line at the bottom.

Again, she pushed the pen across the page.

He straightened the documents, tapping them on the desk top. "Thank you, Laura."

There was dismissal in his voice—a dismissal that made tears surge forth and blur her vision. Is this what their relationship had come down to? she wondered. Cold, impersonal business. Where had the friendliness gone? The intimacy that had been so prevalent before?

The silent questions only mocked her. She *knew* what had happened between them, *knew* she was partly to blame. And that knowledge nearly killed her.

"Dylan, I don't like what's happened between us." The whispered words grated in her throat like lava erupting from a rumbling volcano, hot, harsh and burning.

His ebony eyes narrowed, his jaw tightened. "Don't," he said. "It's better if we don't talk about it."

"Better?" Her gaze widened with disbelief at his statement. "Better than what?"

He looked away, raking his fingers through his raven-black hair.

''Better than avoiding each other?'' she continued. ''Better than ignoring what we had together? Better than—''

''Stop it!'' He stood with such force that his chair rolled backward and smacked into the wall. ''I don't want to argue with you. It tears me up inside. I hate it. Please,'' his voice was ragged, ''I just don't want to fight.''

She searched his face. After a moment, she said softly, ''We don't have to fight. I don't like arguing with you, either. But can't we at least talk? Can't we at least find out what's going on inside each other?''

His face became a mask, an expressionless disguise that hid everything he was feeling. ''It just isn't the right time,'' he said.

Sorrow welled inside her so that her windpipe swelled and her breath caught. Placing her hand at the base of her throat, she swallowed with difficulty. She knew every bit of the raw anguish flaming inside her blatantly showed on her face, in her stance, in her eyes. She didn't care. She wanted Dylan to understand her pain.

He came around his desk, but she noticed that he was very careful not to touch her.

''Don't you think I miss—'' he seemed to search for words ''—what we had? Don't you think I hate the fact that T.C. has come between us?''

A single tear trailed slowly down her face. *Only because you let her.* The silent words screamed inside her head, but her throat was so swollen with emotion she couldn't get them out.

"I don't want us to be like this," he said.

For a moment, Laura was certain that he was going to reach out to her. But he didn't.

His shoulders squared. "But at the same time, I can't help feeling hurt. You betrayed me, Laura. You sided with T.C. You took up her cause without batting an eye—"

"Everything I did and said was for Abbie." Her inhalation was shaky. "Not for you. And not for T.C. But for Abbie."

"I don't believe that," he said. "You argued T.C.'s case too vigorously for me to believe that."

"But, Dylan—"

He cut her off. "Look, I know that the final outcome of the whole thing has been good for Abbie. I'd have to be blind not to see it." He lifted his hand, palm side up. "But that doesn't mean I have to like it."

"I understand that," she murmured.

"I just need time, Laura. This is all so new." He cocked his head to one side. "And not only is it new…it's something I feel I've been forced into."

By me, she silently finished for him. It wasn't necessary that he say it, she knew what he was telling her. The bleak blanket of discouragement that wrapped around her became heavier and heavier.

Was there nothing she could say, nothing she could do to fix things between them? she wondered.

"I just need time," he repeated. "But I will adjust."

There was something in way he said those four little words that made her lift her gaze to his—something in his tone that scratched the outer layer of hopelessness that cocooned her. Had she imagined the hint of optimism in his voice?

He stood a foot from her, his arms tucked tightly across his chest.

"I just need time."

But this time when he made the statement the auspicious quality she'd heard just a moment before was completely gone, and she was left wondering if she'd ever heard it at all. For a split second she'd thought that maybe he'd been trying to imply that, with the passage of time, their relationship might have another chance. But now, looking at his handsome, expressionless face, she had to question if maybe it had been *her own* hope, *her own* desire, that had put some special inflection, some special meaning to his words.

She nodded vaguely, feeling more confused and more frustrated than ever.

All the emotional upheaval she was dealing with was taking its toll. Laura rubbed at her eyes as she rounded the corner on her way back to the day-care center on the first floor of the Mitchell Corporation building. Glancing at her watch, she was relieved to see that the children would be going home soon. She sighed deeply and vowed to spend some quiet time with her son tonight and then get herself a good night's sleep.

She imagined herself tossing and turning as she went over and over every word that Dylan had said in his office just now. She should simply put it out of her head. She knew that. But the practical side of her brain would lose out to the part of her mind that was ruled by her feelings.

The sad thing about it was that she really understood why Dylan felt hurt.

She reached the door of the center and was about to enter when a red-haired man hurried out, brushing past her.

"Sorry," he said, before rushing off down the hall.

Many of the children's parents came to visit at odd times during the day. But Laura didn't remember ever seeing this man before. She thought of speaking to him, but then saw that he was too far away to hear unless she called. Turning back toward the door, she had every intention of going inside. But something stopped her.

She knew that man. She'd seen him somewhere. Although she hadn't seen his face—he'd turned away from her as he passed her, she had this overwhelming feeling that she should remember this man.

A cold shiver tingled along her spine and she frowned. Pressing her fingertips to her lips. She ran back out the door and down the hallway after him.

When she reached the T in the corridor, she looked first one way then the next. Empty. Some silent voice told her to go to the building entrance.

The security guard sat at his desk.

"Did a man just leave here?" Laura asked him. Her heart pounded and she felt breathless with fright for some odd reason.

"A redheaded guy?" The guard seemed calm and cool. "Why, yes, he just left. You want me to try and catch him?"

Was she making more of this than she should? She hadn't even seen the man's face, for heaven's sake.

"No," she hurried to say. "But…uh, could you tell me who he is? Who he came to see?"

"Well, I wasn't here when he signed in, but…let's see…" He looked at the visitor's register. "I can't make out the name." He squinted over the page. "And I can't read the name of the employee he was here to see, either." The guard gazed up at her. "The guy's handwriting is atrocious. Sorry."

"Is it company policy to let just anyone inside the building?" She hated the reprimanding tone of her voice, but every nuance of intuition she had was screaming at her to find out who the red-haired man was and what he was doing in her day-care center.

Why couldn't she remember where she'd seen him before?

"Well, no, ma'am, it isn't." The guard was standing now. "If that guy was here to see an employee, the guard on duty would have had to call that employee and get an okay to let the visitor enter the building. I'm sure Bill followed procedure." The man's face creased with concern. "He's on his break, but I can call him if you like. I can have him come back—"

"No, no," Laura said. "But can I have a look at the register?"

"Sure, Ms. Adams."

He turned the book around so that it faced her.

Placing her finger underneath the signature, she studied the scrawled letters.

"You're right," she murmured to the guard. "His writing is atrocious."

She focused on the first letter of the first name. The whole name was squished together, but could that first one be a capital *V?*

It was hopeless. She couldn't read it.

Her unseeing gaze trailed to the thick glass doors of the front entrance. Suddenly she was back in her hometown of Dewey, dragging her feet in the sand as she spouted off the letters she read from the tattoo on a man's arm.

"Victor." She whispered the name.

Her heart beat so hard that it pained her. Blood

rushed through her ears until she heard nothing but a pounding pulse.

"Dear, God."

"Are you okay, Ms. Adams?"

She looked at the guard. "Have someone from Security meet me at the day care." And she sprinted down the hall.

Chapter Nine

Laura was sprinting so fast she nearly slammed into the glass door of the day-care center before skidding to a halt.

"Okay," she whispered to herself, "just stay calm." Her breath came in gasps that she knew were from both the physical exertion of running and the horrendous anxiety that clawed inside her head. "You don't really know what's happening," she told herself. "You don't want to burst in there and alarm the other children."

But the need to see Abbie, to actually know that she was safe and secure, made Laura shove through the door and hurry directly to the four-year-old room.

The room was quiet and empty, and that startled her. Her mind whirled with frantic thoughts. Where were T.C. and Amy? Where were the children?

The sound of movement in the small coatroom drew her gaze. And when T.C. emerged, Laura bombarded her with questions.

"Where's Amy? And the kids?" she asked. And more pointedly, "Where's Abbie?"

"I told Amy to take the children out to the playground for a little while."

T.C. stood in front of the coatroom door. Her voice sounded…funny, off somehow, and her stance was awkward and stiff. These things registered on the fringes of Laura's subconscious, but her fear regarding Abbie overrode her analytical thinking. "They're outside?"

"It's such a nice afternoon," T.C. explained, "I thought the kids would enjoy some time out in the sunshine."

"Then Abbie's outside with Amy?" Her skin prickled as the words passed her lips. Abbie was outside…the redheaded Victor was outside…. Laura had seen him leave the building, not the premises.

She turned toward the door. She had to get out to the playground. Where the hell was the security guard she'd sent for?

"Actually…she's not with the others."

T.C.'s tentative tone made Laura turn back around. T.C. took a step forward, blatant guilt displayed on her face, in her eyes.

"Where is Abbie?" Laura snapped out the question, feeling that if she didn't get some clear answers she'd lose her mind.

"Here," T.C. admitted quietly, indicating the coatroom behind her with a tilt of her head. "She's right here. Putting her sweater on so she can go outside with the other kids." T.C. moved from in front of the open doorway. "Abbie," she called.

The little girl stepped into sight and the relief that washed over Laura was nearly her undoing. Her legs felt suddenly wobbly and her hands began to tremble. God, it was so good to know Abbie was safe.

"I'm ready, Mommy." Abbie's smile was bright and happy and she evidently didn't notice the tension in the air. "And I buttoned my sweater all by myself."

T.C. knelt down to her daughter's eye level. She smoothed her hand over the front of the sweater that hung cockeyed and uneven. "And you did such a good job."

The praise made one corner of Laura's mouth pull back unwittingly in a small smile. Only a mother would compliment the effort, even if the results of a child's chore were lacking a little.

"I'm sorry," T.C. said, directing her gaze once more on Laura. "Please don't tell Dylan before I have a chance to explain. I can, you know...if you'll only give me a chance...."

The self-reproach in T.C.'s big blue eyes, so like Abbie's, confused Laura for a moment. But then, a thought pierced its way through the anxiety and over-whelming relief that fogged her brain and left her weak: no wonder T.C. was acting awkward and guilt-ridden—for some reason, she'd been alone with Abbie when she *knew* it was expressly forbidden by Dylan.

Laura inhaled a shaky breath and gave T.C. what she hoped was a reassuring smile. Finding T.C. alone with her daughter seemed so trivial a problem compared to the terrifying idea of sighting Abbie's abductor in the building.

And now, discovering that Abbie was safe and sound, and that the only abnormality was that the child wasn't with the rest of the class, Laura was left to wonder if maybe she hadn't misidentified the red-haired man altogether. Maybe the name scrawled in the register had been Vincent, or Vaughan, or Virgil.

She chuckled, all of a sudden feeling light, as though all the negative energy pent up inside her was being discharged. Oh, she still felt too shaky to stand at the moment, but it certainly felt good to know that Abbie wasn't in any danger.

Laura looked at T.C., whose countenance had taken on a bewildered appearance.

"It's okay," Laura said, feeling her smile broaden. "I know you know you're not supposed to be alone with Abbie. I won't say anything to Dylan until we have a chance to talk about it."

The confusion in T.C.'s gaze deepened her eyes

to a dark azure. But quickly—too quickly—they cleared.

"R-right," she stammered. "I'll tell you all about it."

Laura's smile died a swift death. There was something unnatural and abrupt in T.C.'s demeanor—something that had nothing to do with her being caught alone with Abbie.

Just then the child tugged on her mother's sleeve.

"Mommy," Abbie complained plaintively, "I want to go out on the swings."

Unable to take her eyes from T.C.'s face, Laura tried to figure out why she felt something about this scene was off kilter. Why did she feel that—

"Mommy." Abbie's voice took on a whining quality.

T.C. swiveled her head to look down at her daughter. And Laura's breath actually stopped as she watched the woman's short, silky hair fan out from her head and swing into her face. The set of that chin...the tilt of those shoulders...

Laura's mouth went dry. Suddenly, for the second time in the past quarter hour, she was back on the beach in Dewey, seeing the fleeing man with the frizzy red hair grab the hand of his accomplice. All those weeks ago her hair had been long and flowing and had swung out in a wide-arcing curtain. Laura remembered how the sun had glinted off the glorious blond tresses. She remembered describing the woman's beautiful flaxen hair to the police.

Laura looked at the young woman standing before her—the young woman she'd befriended—the young woman she'd sacrificed so much for—and her heart ached with such pain she thought that she would surely cry out from the agony.

"It was you," she whispered, for her voice could do no more than that. "On the beach."

T.C.'s eyes became moist with tears of panic. "Laura, let me take Abbie out to Amy and the other children. I'll come right back and explain everything."

"Don't take that child out of this room." Laura was surprised how firm her tone became. "Don't take her out of my sight."

T.C.'s shoulders sagged. "You really don't believe I'd do anything to hurt Abbie, do you?" She swallowed. "Laura, I love my daughter."

Just then a security guard poked his head into the room.

"Ms. Adams?" he called, looking expectantly at Laura. "Someone said you might have some trouble here."

Laura raised herself up from the chair. "It wasn't as bad as I had expected," she told him, wondering if she was lying to the man. "But I do need you. Would you mind escorting Abbie out to the playground with her friends and then stay there until I come out?''

There were questions in his eyes, but he automatically answered, ''Certainly.''

''But, Mommy, I want you to come with me.'' It was clear from the look on Abbie's face that she didn't understand what was going on between Laura and her mother.

''It's okay, honey,'' T.C. said. ''I need to talk to Laura. You go on out and play.''

The guard smiled down at Abbie and took her by the hand, leading her out the door. Laura could hear him engaging the child in friendly conversation as the sound of their voices faded down the hall.

''Laura,'' T.C. said as she approached the table, ''you do believe that I'd never harm Abbie.''

T.C. had made it a statement, but Laura could tell from her tone that she wanted an answer...or at least a response.

''To tell you the truth,'' Laura admitted, ''I don't know what to believe anymore.''

T.C. eased herself into a child-sized chair across the table from Laura.

After a moment of tense silence, Laura said, ''Talk to me.''

It was obvious that T.C. was ill at ease and reluctant to speak.

''It's true,'' she finally said. ''I was there on the

beach that day…with Victor.'' She hesitated. ''Victor's my brother. My half brother.''

''So, he *was* here today.'' It wasn't a question. A burst of anger rose up inside Laura, sharp and piercing. ''How could you do such a thing? How could you frighten that child the way you did? That's your daughter!''

T.C.'s eyes were pleading. ''I wanted to see Abbie. Laura, I hadn't seen her…held her since she was a baby. My need to be with her—even if it was only for a moment—became so urgent. Abbie was all I thought about. I couldn't sleep, couldn't eat.''

She clasped her hands together tightly. ''It got to the point that I was watching the house every day. I noticed that Mr. Mitchell, Dylan's father, started taking Abbie out every Saturday.'' Her chin dipped as she admitted, ''I followed them one weekend to Dewey.'' She lifted her eyes to Laura. ''And I started going there every Saturday. It somehow made me feel closer to my daughter.''

''And how did Victor fit into all of this?'' Laura asked.

''He just wants me to be happy.'' T.C.'s mouth curled into a tiny smile. ''He's my brother. We've been through a lot together. He loves me.''

Laura saw from T.C.'s countenance that there was more to be told about Victor. She simply waited.

T.C. lifted one hand and rubbed her knuckles lightly across her chin as though carefully contemplating what she wanted to say—how much she wanted to divulge.

Finally, her shoulders settled with determination, seemingly coming to some conclusion.

"We did talk about taking Abbie," T.C. confessed.

Disappointment escaped from Laura in a hiss.

"But I decided against it," she quickly added. "Victor only wanted me to be happy. He only suggested it because he thought that's what I wanted." She squeezed and kneaded the palm of one hand with the fingers of the other. "Laura, you've got to believe me when I say that I never wanted to hurt Dylan. I never would have taken Abbie from him, from the nice home he provided her, the wonderful life he gives…"

"But why would you and your brother want to frighten her so?" Laura couldn't hold back the question.

"I was desperate."

"Desperate?" She allowed every ounce of hostility she was feeling to be conveyed in her voice. "You had no idea if there was even a reason to feel desperate. You didn't even try to approach Dylan about seeing Abbie—"

"Come on, Laura," T.C. cut her off. "You know how he feels about me."

"All I know is," Laura said, "there is a right way

to do things and there's a wrong way. And, time and again, you've chosen the wrong way.''

''What do you mean, time and again?'' Her question was softly spoken, almost meek. ''I know that Victor and I were wrong to do what we did in Dewey—''

''You tried to abduct Abbie!'' Laura's tone held so much incredulity that it raised an octave. ''I'd—''

''But I didn't!'' T.C. interjected with feeling. ''I wasn't trying to *take* her. I only wanted to *talk* to her. To meet her. I wouldn't have taken her from the beach. I told you that.''

''You expect me to believe that? I was there, T.C. I saw how scared Abbie was. I was there.''

T.C. only looked at her sadly before saying, ''I wasn't going to take her.''

''And then to think, after the Dewey fiasco failed, you came here. You manipulated your way into the day care. You manipulated me.'' That was what really hurt Laura the most. The fact that T.C. had used her.

''Dylan was right all along,'' Laura said quietly. ''You used this job, you used me—''

''Oh, no, Laura,'' T.C. cried. ''Please don't say that.''

''How can I not? It's the truth.''

Laura sat there, actually feeling surprised and completely overtaken by the magnitude of her anger. She'd known for some time now that T.C. had been

dishonest when she'd sought this job in the day care;
she'd known that T.C. had procured employment to
be near her daughter. Yes, Laura had known the situation, had even realized why T.C. had done what
she'd done. In fact, it was because she'd understood
T.C.'s motives that she'd pressed Dylan so hard to
allow Abbie to continue coming to the day care.

Why, then, was she feeling the desire to lash out
at T.C.? Why was she feeling so hurt, so infuriated
to find out that T.C. had made yet another mistake?
What had Laura so confused, she knew, was the fact
that even though another horrendous act of T.C.'s
was coming to light, Laura still understood the
woman's motives. Laura could still rationalize a loving mother's desperate desire to know her daughter.

"I know that Victor shouldn't have come here today."

T.C.'s soft words snapped Laura back to the present.

"But he's waited so long to meet Abbie. And he
feels so bad about making her cry on the beach this
past summer."

"He *should* feel bad." Laura's anger spilled from
her in the form of harsh words. Surely because she
understood T.C.'s motives didn't make her any less
irate. "He was stupid to try and scare Abbie off the
beach. *He* was stupid—" her voice fluttered "—and
you were stupid. And I don't know when Dylan will

say when he discovers that you and your half-brother were behind the whole thing.''

T.C.'s blue-eyed gaze lowered. ''What if we didn't tell him?'' she murmured.

Laura heaved a weary sigh. ''You know that's impossible. I can't keep something like this from him.''

With her eyes still glued to the floor, T.C. nodded her understanding.

''Dear Lord,'' Laura moaned, ''how could you continue to make such bad decisions, T.C.?''

The young woman must have realized the question was rhetorical because she remained silent.

Shifting in the small wooden seat, Laura thought about actually having to tell Dylan what she'd learned and a shiver shuttered through her. He'd been so angry when he'd found out about T.C. getting herself hired by Mitchell Corporation, Laura had no idea how he'd react to this turn of events.

Maybe it wouldn't be too bad, she tried to tell herself. Maybe because the whole business had happened weeks ago... Maybe, just maybe...

Who was she trying to kid? She knew Dylan would be absolutely furious.

Almost as though reading her thoughts, T.C. asked, ''What do you think Dylan will do when he finds out?''

''I'm more than certain he'll be...upset.'' Then her breath rushed past her lips and her eyes rolled heavenward. ''Hell, he'll be more than upset.''

Nibbling on her bottom lip, T.C. sought Laura's eyes with her own. "I want you to know that I realize how I've come between you and Dylan. You've been so good not to make me feel bad about the rift I've caused between the two of you. And I want you to know that I'm sorry."

Laura smoothed her hand across her forehead. "I was doing what I thought was right. I felt that you and Abbie needed time together. You two needed to know each other. That's what was right." She inhaled deeply. "I only hope that from now on you, too, will do what's right."

"If Dylan will allow me to," T.C. commented sadly.

Reaching out, Laura touched her fingertips to the young woman's forearm. "Dylan's going to be angry," she said. "He'll be furious to find out what you've done. But the right thing to do is face his anger, face the consequences of your actions... whatever those consequences may be."

After a moment, T.C. whispered, "I'm afraid."

Laura nodded. "So am I."

"Will you tell him for me?"

Without hesitation, she nodded again. She'd already decided it would be best if she were the one to take the brunt of Dylan's anger. Maybe that's why she'd felt so angry at T.C. Laura hated the thought of facing Dylan with this news. But she also felt that if he focused all his hostility on her, then Abbie and

T.C. might still have some slim chance of having a relationship.

She might as well take his anger regarding the situation, she thought ruefully, because she knew from past experience with Dylan that she'd surely take the blame.

Abbie sat still and quiet beside Laura as they waited just outside Dylan's office. Laura's veins felt frozen with icy apprehension as she contemplated Dylan's reaction to what she would tell him.

I hold you personally responsible. His threat echoed over and over in her head. And Laura had taken on that responsibility willingly, because she was that certain that Abbie should know her mother. But now, after finding out what T.C. had done, how the young woman had made poor choice after poor choice, Laura's certainty waned. She felt confused. She didn't know what was right anymore.

She knew without a doubt that the things T.C. had done were dead wrong. But at the same time, she also knew that T.C. was most probably right in her assessment that, had she asked, Dylan wouldn't have allowed her anywhere near Abbie. It had been Laura who had intervened and persuaded him against his will to let T.C. have some time with Abbie.

And it had been that forceful persuasion that had destroyed the budding relationship Laura and Dylan had been developing.

"Are you mad at me?"

Laura glanced over to see Abbie staring at her with big, rounded blue eyes.

"Oh, no, honey," Laura said. "I'm not angry with you."

"Are you mad at my mommy?" The child lifted her hand and worried the tip of her index finger with her tiny white teeth.

Laura couldn't help but hesitate as she pondered an answer. How could she explain to a four-year-old her feelings regarding T.C.'s actions when she couldn't quite work them out for herself?

"Abbie, I don't want you to worry," she finally said. "Everything's going to work out." She smoothed her palm over the child's silky, flaxen hair. "You'll see."

"Will I get to go to the day care?" Abbie's deep anxiety gathered in her eyes in the form of brimming tears. "Will I get to play with my mommy?"

Laura's heart nearly ripped in two. This little girl had no idea what was happening. She didn't know about the terrible, dishonorable lengths her mother had gone to, she didn't understand that Laura and her father were only concerned with her welfare. All Abbie perceived was that, for some reason, there was a chance that her mother would be taken away from her.

Gathering Abbie onto her lap, Laura hugged her tight. "Abbie, I don't want you to worry. Your mommy and your daddy will work this out. They both love you very much.''

It was such a complicated situation, one that would take Abbie years and years to understand. Laura knew that—knew it was fruitless to try and explain. So for now, all she could do for the child was to assuage her fears, tell her that everything would be okay, and then hope she wasn't lying.

"Mr. Mitchell is off the phone now." Dylan's secretary gently interrupted Laura's hugging session. "He can see you now."

"Thank you," Laura told the woman. Then to Abbie she said, "I want you to stay right here and wait for me, okay?"

"Abbie will be fine," the secretary commented brightly. "We'll get us some paper and a pencil. And look what I have for you."

"A lollipop." Abbie's sad little face lit with delight.

"Would you like orange flavor or cherry?"

Laura didn't hear Abbie's answer as she walked to the closed door of Dylan's office. Her stomach seized up with cold, empty dread. There would be no easy way to tell him what she had to say. So she'd just do it, she thought, in clear and simple terms.

A well-thought-out plan usually helped to execute a task, but still Laura noticed how her hand shook as she raised it to knock on the door.

"Come."

The frosty sound of Dylan's voice made her uneasiness freeze into a solid block of icy panic. She didn't want to do this.

Laura turned the knob and eased open the door. He held up his hand, palm out, a clear message that he wanted her silence as he scribbled furiously on a pad of lined paper that sat in front of him. He put down his pen.

"I'm sorry," he said, finally looking up at her. "I had to get those numbers down from that phone call." He stood up. "I was told that Abbie is with you. Is she hurt?"

"Oh, no," she quickly assured him. "But I brought Abbie with me because...well, you see...I found something out today."

His brow raised in silent query.

She swallowed, and moistened her lips with her tongue. She inhaled deeply and gathered every fiber of inner strength she possessed. "I need to tell you about it, and I'd feel better if you sat down... relaxed." She took a seat opposite him and tried to become as tranquil as possible.

He eased himself down in his chair, his forehead creasing deeply. "Sounds pretty serious. You're certain Abbie's okay?"

"Oh, yes," she said. Then she told him her story. The clear, unadorned truth. She spoke quietly and calmly, but she did talk as quickly as she could in order to get it all out before he responded.

As she talked, her stomach grew tense, her hands clutched in her lap at the sight of his face...his eyes. Though his reaction was silent, it was unmistakable. His shoulder muscles strained against his cotton dress shirt, his jaw became rigid. Anger sharpened every plane and angle of his handsome face. But it was his eyes that were the most revealing.

Storms brewed in the black depths of his obsidian gaze. They sparked with the lightning of barely suffused emotion. And with each piece of information she disclosed, his eyes became more and more thunderous. Until, finally, the torrent broke.

"I told you that woman was no good."

Laura flinched as the harsh words grated from his throat.

"I told you, and you refused to listen. You insisted on putting her *maternal needs*—"

He actually sneered the phrase at her, and Laura felt her spine straighten with indignation.

"—above my warnings. And now, the truth comes out. Now her true character comes to light."

Trying to remain calm, Laura fought the ominous narrowing of her eyes. She had *known* he was going to find some way to blame her for this.

"If you hadn't talked me into sending Abbie to the day care in the first place—" he threw the censure at her "—then my daughter wouldn't have been exposed to that woman."

"*That woman* is Abbie's mother," she reminded him sharply.

His lips twisted with disgust as he said, "*That woman* isn't fit to be anyone's mother."

Laura smacked her palm down on the arm of the high-backed chair. "You haven't even taken the time to get to know T.C. How do you know whether or not she's fit?"

Pain flickered across his features and he leaned back in his chair. His voice was dead calm as he commented, "I can't believe after all she's done that you would still side with her over me."

She felt the blood drain from her face. Is that what she'd done? Sided with T.C. again? She had.

But why? she wondered. Especially when she had been so upset by the discovery that T.C. had been behind the Dewey Beach episode.

It was because she'd felt a need to strike out at Dylan for saying "I told you so." She wanted to make him realize that he was making rash judgments where T.C. was concerned. He continued to act on his emotions and not on logical thinking. But even though she felt all these things she shouldn't have taken T.C.'s part. She shouldn't have sided with the woman.

Laura's throat squeezed shut with some emotion she couldn't name. Why couldn't he understand that she wanted to be on *his* side in all of this? Why didn't he see that she wanted the two of them to be working together in Abbie's best interests?

"I'm sorry." An honest apology was her only recourse. "I was just as angry to learn about what T.C. had done as you are." She inhaled deeply. "But let's try and remember that nothing terrible has happened here. It's just that we found another piece of the puzzle that makes up T.C.'s past. She's trying to change. I truly believe that she loves Abbie. She wants to do what's right where your daughter is concerned."

Dylan remained silent, his lips pressed into a thin, disapproving line.

Seeing the face of this man—the man she'd come to love so dearly—Laura realized that he would never be able to get over the feeling that she'd betrayed him. She felt an overwhelming urge to cry. She felt her chin quiver, but she held the tears at bay.

"Dylan, you have to know that through this whole thing with T.C.," she said, hearing the pleading quality to her voice, "I've only been urging you to do what's right for Abbie. It may not have been the best thing for you, I realize that. And it's been hard for you, I realize that, too." Her tone became quiet. "But it was a wonderful thing…your letting Abbie be with her mother."

Laura directed her gaze away from his dark, hawk-like eyes. "After finding out everything I have about T.C., I've come to the conclusion that…maybe you've been right all along. Maybe T.C. isn't the best influence on a young child.''

He leaned forward and rested his elbows on the desk top, his eyes becoming even more piercing as he studied her.

''A-and although,'' she stammered, ''I do believe that T.C. would never do anything to harm Abbie, and that she loves her dearly—'' she stopped long enough to swallow ''—I feel that T.C. has made some really bad choices.''

She had to force herself not to voice all the very valid reasons behind those poor choices.

''And,'' she went on, ''I want you to know that I'll go along with any decision you make about this. If you want to keep Abbie from the day care, so be it. If you want me to fire T.C.—'' she hesitated for the barest of moments ''—then I will.''

Leaning forward, she placed her fingertips on the very edge of his desk. ''All I ask is that you think about it first. And talk to Abbie about your decision. Talk to her and try to understand how she feels.''

There was a knock at the door and Dylan's secretary dipped her head into the room.

''I found some felt-tipped pens for Abbie,'' the woman said, looking around the room. She frowned. ''Where is she?''

Panic rose up inside Laura like a sharp-fanged cobra. ''I left her out there with you,'' she said.

"She's gone?" There was a cutting edge on Dylan's question.

"Well..." The secretary looked back over her shoulder.

"How long has she been gone?" he asked.

"I was only in the file room for a few moments," the woman said.

"She has to have gone back to the day care," Laura said. "Back to her mother."

Without another word, Laura picked up the phone and dialed the telephone number for the day-care center. She spoke with one of the teachers, and with each word her heart became heavier and heavier. She gently replaced the receiver in its cradle.

"T.C.'s gone," she whispered. "They can't find her anywhere."

Chapter Ten

Dylan felt as though he were being blindsided by a kaleidoscope of colliding emotions. He looked at Laura, her hand still on the telephone receiver.

Her story concerning Abbie's attempted kidnapping had thrown him onto some wildly careering emotional roller-coaster ride. He'd felt astonished by her revelation, and angry—no, furious—that T.C. would do such a thing. His feelings had dipped and twisted with bewilderment and confusion as he listened to Laura, but before he could get things straight in his head, his emotions whipped him one way then another with irritation, exasperation and rage.

And on top of all this, he'd just learned that his daughter wasn't where she was supposed to be. She was gone. Missing. And from what Laura had said, so was T.C.

His gaze sought and held Laura's. He wanted to tell her all the things he was feeling. He wanted to confide in her all the turmoil tossing inside him. But at the moment he couldn't seem to put two coherent words together. He couldn't figure out why, he thought derisively, he'd certainly been able to say plenty just a few seconds ago. He'd found no problem at all in foisting all the ridicule and blame he felt on Laura.

"Okay," she said, "so T.C. has taken Abbie."

She said the words almost to herself, as though she was working out the situation in her own head.

"I never would have thought it," she continued softly. "I can hardly believe that she'd do something like this."

He felt the need to say something, but his brain seemed on overload to the point that he couldn't speak.

After a moment of thick silence, Laura glared at him.

"I know," she snapped at him. "You hold me personally responsible." She moved swiftly to the door of his office.

"Laura, wait," he was finally able to say.

He couldn't remember why at the moment, but he knew Abbie was safe. Knew that T.C. couldn't have taken her out of the building.

"I'll find them." She nearly shouted at him. "If it's the last thing I do."

"Laura," he called to her again. But she was gone.

Dylan felt an overwhelming urge to close himself off from the world and sort through all the feelings that were coursing through his body at breakneck speed. Sitting across from Laura, listening to her story, he'd come to some stark conclusions. Conclusions that needed his full, undivided attention.

But first he needed to take care of the most pressing problem—Abbie's whereabouts. Abbie had slipped off, and T.C. couldn't be found.

Taking a deep, calming breath, he picked up the phone and dialed Security. He knew he needn't worry about T.C. taking their daughter off-site. He'd alerted Security about the situation the day that he'd discovered T.C. was working for the day care.

Not exactly the same day, he ruefully remembered. It was the day after, the morning following Laura's tirade in the garage when she'd pushed and pushed him to bring Abbie to the center.

After explaining the circumstances to the head of the security department, Dylan said, "Find them. Then call me."

He put down the phone and settled in his chair to wait. His security people were good at what they did; Dylan knew he wouldn't have to wait long.

The thought that Abbie might slip off to be with her mother made him realize how his daughter felt. Laura had told him Abbie was upset, worried that Laura was "mad" at T.C. Dylan was certain that his daughter, with her four-year-old reasoning skills, somehow equated Laura's anger against her mother with the possibility of T.C. losing her job at the day-care center. He was also sure that his past behavior— taking her away from the center in an angry huff— also contributed to her fretting.

Do what's right for Abbie, not what's right for you. Laura's message echoed in his brain.

The beautiful woman with the rich, chestnut hair who had come into his life like a runaway train threatened to take over his thoughts altogether. But he held her at bay. He needed to work out his feelings regarding his daughter and T.C. Then he'd focus all his energy on Laura.

The telephone rang and he snatched up the receiver.

After listening a moment, he remarked, "Good work. Bring them both to my office." Without hesitation, he added, "And find Ms. Adams, would you? Escort her up here also." He frowned when he thought of how she'd left. "She may need a little gentle persuasion, but get her up here."

He rang off, then worriedly rubbed his fingers along his jaw. He felt as though he was seeing the truth about a lot of things for the first time. Why hadn't he seen it before? he wondered. Laura had certainly tried to make him face the facts of the matter. He almost chuckled as he pictured her luscious mouth pursed with righteous indignation as she'd lectured him. Why hadn't he realized she'd only been spelling out the truth?

Hell, who was he kidding? He'd refused to see the truth. He wasn't a stupid man, he knew that. And it irritated him to think that he'd let his pride—

He cut off the thought. This was not time to worry about the past. He'd done too much of that already. He needed to focus on the future. He needed to make plans for the days and weeks and years ahead. His mind churned with the possibilities.

What had to be done wasn't going to be easy for him.

Do what's best for Abbie...what's best for Abbie... Laura's soft, gentle voice intruded on his thoughts yet again. He shook his head. No, this wasn't going to be easy.

But he had to do what was right. For Abbie, for her mother. However, he didn't feel that that situation would be too hard to solve. It seemed that the only hurdle everyone was facing was his damned male pride. Dylan ran agitated fingers through his already disheveled hair. No, he felt pretty certain that between himself, T.C. and Abbie, they could work out a reasonable agreement.

It was the situation with Laura that concerned him the most.... He saw things so clearly now...his feelings for this woman. And how unfairly he'd treated her. Hell, he'd really screwed up their relationship royally.

The thing to do was to bare his soul to Laura, he knew that. But at this point, after all the stupid things he'd said and done, he was left wondering if she still cared enough to listen.

Laura felt as though the world were crashing in on her. If she had been a weaker person, she'd have allowed herself the luxury of sitting right down and crying her heart out.

She'd thought that Alfred Mitchell had given her the means to achieve her dreams when he'd bequeathed to her a portion of Mitchell Corporation. She'd thought building a corporate day-care center— a *successful* corporate day-care center—would make her happy. She'd thought her goal would better her life, and her son's life.

But now, even though she'd acquired her dream, she truly believed that she would have been better off if she'd never heard of Mitchell Corporation, if she'd never met Alfred Mitchell, or Dylan, if she'd stayed in Dewey Beach with her tiny, in-home day care.

How could someone mess up her life so thoroughly? she wondered. How could she lose her heart to a man who was so blinded by bitterness and anger about his past that he couldn't see the here and now? Couldn't see how much he was loved—by his daughter, by the people around him, by Laura herself?

It made her so sad to think that she and Dylan

didn't have a chance of being together. Not after she'd gone against him time and time again where T.C. and Abbie were concerned. The fact that she was only following her conscience was irrelevant. She'd lost Dylan. She'd lost her chance at a relationship with him.

Her heart felt caught in a vise...squeezed by some invisible clamp of cold steel. She wouldn't let herself cry. She couldn't. Not after that fervent promise she'd made to find his daughter.

The late-afternoon sun was bright in the parking lot, the autumnal breeze cool against her skin as she searched for T.C.'s car. The idea to look for the automobile had come to Laura as she'd rushed from Dylan's office. With her mind churning over possibilities of where T.C. and Abbie might be, Laura had reasoned that if T.C.'s car was where it should be, then that lessened the chances that the woman had left the premises with Abbie.

"There." She breathed the word to herself, relief flooding through her whole body when she actually saw T.C.'s small, pale yellow hatchback neatly parked between the crisp, white lines.

But then it dawned on her that T.C. could have left with her brother. Victor *had* been in the building earlier. Her hopes plummeted and a heavy dread returned to weigh her down with worry and fear.

A car passed Laura slowly and she realized that Mitchell Corporation employees were leaving for the day. She scanned the parking lot. It would be so easy to miss T.C. if she really meant to take Abbie.

Laura recognized that if she was to find them, she needed help. Maybe after all the children had gone home, she could convince the teachers to help her scour every inch of the building. Then Laura was pleased and relieved to see a security guard heading straight toward her.

"I need your help," she called, hating the nervous tension in her voice.

"I'd like to help you, Ms. Adams," he told her when he got close, "but I've been instructed to escort you to Mr. Mitchell's office."

Laura's brow knit with confusion. "But there must be some mistake. I just came from there."

The guard shrugged. "All I know is that I've been asked to take you upstairs."

Her obstinate streak reared its ugly head. She didn't know why Dylan wanted to see her, or why he felt he needed to send Security to escort her to his office, but she had no intention of going anywhere with this man.

"I'm sorry, but I can't go right now." She turned and took a step.

She was more than mildly surprised when he stopped her with a light hand on her forearm.

"Ms. Adams, I really wish you'd come with me."

She eyed his hand with a raised brow and he lifted it as though she'd scorched his skin with her gaze.

"I understand your dilemma," she said, "but I'm right in the middle of something. I can't go to see Mr. Mitchell right at this moment—" she kept her tone as pleasant as she could but firm enough to brook no argument "—but you can tell him I will come to his office as soon as it's possible for me to do so."

The guard actually squirmed with discomfort and indecision. "Well, Ms. Adams...you see...I haven't been on this job but a couple of weeks." He gave a long-suffering sigh. "I'd hate to lose it...just 'cause you refused to take a short walk up to Mr. Mitchell's office."

Laura fumed. How dare the great Dylan Mitchell summon her to him? And to send this poor, pitiful man to do the job! Why, she'd give Dylan a thing or two to think about.

"Fine," she snapped. "I'll go."

The guard's wide mouth cocked into a lopsided grin. "Thank you, ma'am."

"Oh, you people are so well trained," Laura muttered as she stomped across the asphalt.

"Ma'am?"

"If you can't bully me, you'll make me feel so sorry for you I can't help but do what you ask."

The guard hitched up his trousers. "Whatever gets the job done," he commented proudly.

The elevator ride was made in silence and when

the door slid open, Laura said, "I can make it from here on my own."

"I'll just go along, if you don't mind."

Oh, she thought, Dylan will pay for this humiliating experience. She'd been holding back her fury for weeks now. He could do what he wanted about the situation with T.C., but Laura refused to allow him to treat her in such a degrading manner. The high and mighty Dylan would hear every angry word she felt.

Laura savored the rage, fed on it. Because it was easier to feel furious about the way he treated her than to feel hurt and sorry to know that she'd lost him.

Dylan's secretary was just gathering her purse and jacket on her way out of the office. Laura was too angry to speak to the woman. She stalked passed her and pushed open Dylan's office door.

"Dylan Mitchell," she said in a loud clear voice, "who do you think you are, to send—"

The words died midstream as she took in the sight before her.

T.C. had obviously been brought into the room with Abbie just moments before Laura. Abbie looked upset and frightened. T.C. was on the verge of tears. At the sight of Laura, T.C. exclaimed, "I never left the building. I'm sorry they couldn't find me. Abbie came to me crying and—"

She tried to move toward Laura, but the security

guard tightened his hold on her arm. A sob broke from T.C.'s throat.

"That's my mommy!" Abbie kicked the guard in the shin and then ran behind her father's legs. "Daddy, tell him to stop hurting my mommy."

There was a split second of heavy silence before Dylan spoke.

"You can go," he told the guard who was holding T.C. Then he turned his gaze to the man who had followed Laura into the room and nodded a dismissal at him also.

Dylan's dark eyes locked onto Laura for a moment, and she couldn't be certain, but she thought she read... He turned to his daughter before she could capture the emotion.

She watched as he bent and picked up Abbie.

"Now, listen here," he said gently. "I don't want you to worry about a thing."

Abbie's teary eyes grew wide with sadness. "But I don't want you to be mad at mommy."

Dylan's lips tilted into a kind smile. "I'm not angry with T.C.," he said. "You can come to see her in the day care every day."

The child remained silent, as though she wasn't sure she believed what her father was saying.

He looked over at T.C.

"I was only trying to comfort Abbie," T.C. rushed to say in her own defense. "You didn't have to send

Security. I was on my way up to your office with her.''

"I know you were,'' he said. "And we can work this out. The two of us,'' he added pointedly. "We don't need Laura as a mediator.'' He adjusted Abbie on his hip. "Why don't you come to the house to-night…say around seven-thirty, and we'll work out some kind of visitation agreement.''

"Y-you really mean it?'' T.C.'s question was tentative, as though she was gun-shy.

Dylan nodded. "I mean it, and I'm sorry I've been such an ass about the whole thing.''

Suddenly he clamped his lips shut, seemingly refusing to say another word on the subject. He put Abbie down. "You go with your mother now,'' he told his daughter. "I'll pick you up at the day care in a little while.''

"Okay, daddy.'' Abbie tucked her little hand in T.C.'s and they went out the door together.

Laura was shocked by what she'd heard. The words that had come out of Dylan's mouth were so opposed to everything he'd said and done up to this point. She stood there as though on pins and needles, simply waiting for the next surprise.

"Close the door, Laura.'' His voice was whisper-soft. "We need to talk.''

She didn't move. She'd come up here meaning to unload all her anger and frustration on him. But suddenly she realized that she wasn't angry any longer.

She had no idea where the bad feelings had gone, but somehow they had dissipated into thin air.

The reason probably had something to do with the fact that Dylan's attitude had changed. His high-and-mighty disposition had altered, had transformed into something…softer. She'd seen it clearly when he'd talked with his daughter, and with T.C.

She didn't know what had happened to…change him, but she felt…awed by the change.

"Laura."

He said her name a second time and the rich, deep timbre of his voice woke her from her musings.

"Close the door, please," he repeated.

She did as he bid.

"Let's sit down."

He moved to the leather couch that sat on one side of the room. She eased herself down, feeling hazy, almost as though she were moving in dreamlike slow motion.

"I do realize what an ass I've been," he said.

She had enough wits about her to murmur, "Hear, hear."

He chuckled. "I can always count on you to be absolutely honest about your feelings. I've missed that."

Laura felt an overwhelming urge to pinch herself, to see if she was awake, to see if this was real.

"What's going on?" She blurted out the question

without thinking how it sounded. "What's happened to you, Dylan? Are you feeling all right?"

His chuckle turned into a full-fledged laugh. "Lord, but you're gorgeous," he said.

His eyes turned suddenly serious and he reached out and touched her hair.

Her back stiffened. "Dylan, you'd better tell me what's happened to you." Her bewilderment forced her to add, "You're...different. What's happened?"

He drew back his hand, a tiny smile tugging at the corners of his mouth. "You," he said softly. "You happened to me."

Reaching up, he traced the crease that wrinkled her brow. "You came into my life when I was dealing with so many bad things—my father's death, my new position as president of Mitchell Corporation...." His fingers trailed along her jawline. "And you brought some big problems with you."

Laura was taken aback. "I did?"

He grinned ruefully. "Well, that's not quite true. The problems were already here—you simply pointed them out."

His delicate caress traveled the length of her neck and then up to her ear. Her skin tingled in the wake of his touch, so much so that it was hard for her to keep her mind on the conversation.

"You hadn't been here but a few days," he continued, "before pointing out what a lousy father I was being. You told me that I was a workaholic who needed to spend more time with his daughter.'' His eyes twinkled. "You saw an injustice and you felt compelled to right it."

"You make me sound like some kind of lunatic superhero," she muttered.

"Oh, no," he assured her. "That's not what I mean at all. You made my life and my daughter's life better by speaking up."

"All I had to do was point out your...deficiency," her face flushed at the use of the noun, "but you changed your relationship with Abbie all by yourself. And besides," she added, "I probably wouldn't have said a word if we hadn't been trying to figure out the cryptic message Alfred left us in his letter."

"I'm not so sure of that," he said. "You're unique, Laura. You're the kind of person who makes great hero material."

Laura's face screwed up with disbelief. "What in the world are you talking about?"

"I'm talking about this crazy, mixed-up situation with T.C." His fingertip ever so gently investigated the outline of her ear. "You knew that Abbie wanted and needed to know her mother. And despite the fact that I...couldn't seem to come to terms with the predicament—" his face grew full of regret "—hell, let's face it, I didn't want to deal with it at all. I was embarrassed by the fact that I'd been taken in by a..."

His hand dropped to her shoulder as his breath left

him in a rush. "I'm through with name-calling and blaming T.C. for my actions," he said. "I simply need to deal with things as they stand. And that's what I intend to do."

He stared deeply into her eyes. "But I do need to tell you that I was ashamed for you to know that all those years ago I had let my—" he hesitated, searching for the right words "—the lower regions of my body destroy rational thought. I was so self-conscious about it, in fact, that I could hardly face you. Could hardly talk to you. I thought you wouldn't want to have anything to do with me after finding out about the mistake I made."

"But, Dylan, we all make mistakes in our lives."

For a moment they were quiet. He slid his fingertips up the curve of her neck. The silky heat of his skin on hers was enticing, and Laura loved it. But the importance of the conversation at hand forced her to speak.

"I thought you blamed me," she said softly. "It angered me to think that you did."

"I probably did," he admitted. "I blamed you. I blamed T.C. And anyone else who came to mind." A soft, disgusted sound passed from his lips. "Simply because I couldn't seem to face the blame myself. But I do understand now. I do realize that T.C. is a part of my past—a part that must be dealt with. Without her, I wouldn't have Abbie. And T.C. does love Abbie. Just as much as I do." He smiled gently. "It took me a long time, but I finally do understand all that you tried to tell me.'' His smile widened to a grin. ''I'm just thick-skulled.''

He shifted his body so that he was closer to her, continuing to caress her face and neck. ''The amazing thing is that even though I gave you such a hard time about the whole situation, and even though you kept finding out little bits about T.C.—how she lied to get the job, and then that she was at Dewey Beach...'' He let the sentence trail off. ''But all the while you did what you thought was best for Abbie.''

Laura nodded. ''I really did believe that Abbie should know her mother. I'm not saying that T.C. should have custody, or that she should take Abbie off for long periods of time—I don't think she's proved herself mature enough for that. But I do think that they should have some kind of relationship.''

''I agree,'' he said. ''And it was that belief of yours that turned the situation around. You did what you thought was right for Abbie even though it wasn't the easiest thing for you.''

''It was terrible for me,'' she blurted out without thinking.

Now it was his turn to look concerned, but he remained quiet as he waited for her to explain.

''In trying to help Abbie and T.C. get together,'' she began slowly, ''I nearly ruined our relationship.''

''It wasn't you,'' he whispered his assurance. ''It was me. And T.C. You fell into this mess. And you stuck with us until we got ourselves straightened out.'' His head tilted slightly. ''If you don't know it, Laura Adams, I need to tell you that I love you more than words can say.''

Her heart skipped a beat before shifting into overdrive to race in her chest. She'd wanted to hear those words for so long, had waited to hear them.

''And I love you,'' she answered.

She was relieved that she got the statement out before her throat closed with emotion that was deep enough to bring tears to her eyes.

He pulled her to him and buried his face in her hair. ''Don't cry,'' he whispered huskily. ''I never want to make you cry.''

''These are happy tears.'' But her voice sounded so ridiculously squeaky that they both ended up laughing.

He kissed her then, a long, sensuous kiss that seemed to stop time itself. His lips were warm and moist and they conveyed every ounce of passion he was feeling.

His warm palm cupped her breast and fanned the embers of desire deep inside her body. Laura slipped into his embrace, onto his lap and returned his kiss. She let the fires that had been banked inside her flare white hot. She wanted this man, she loved him. And now it was safe to show him just how much.

Epilogue

Laura gazed down at her hand where it was splayed on the sun-warmed sand. As many times as she'd seen that dazzling diamond wedding band there on the third finger of her left hand, its sparkle still stirred in her a warm, tingling rush of happiness. It was hard for her to believe that she and Dylan had been married nearly two years now, and her heart still thumped a heavy beat at the mere thought of the man.

A shriek of laughter drew her attention to the shoreline where Dylan and Brian frantically scooped the wet sand with their cupped hands. These weekends at Dewey Beach were wonderful. She and Dylan had found a small cottage right near the beach where they could relax and enjoy themselves and their children.

Her lips curled into a contented smile and she looked over to where the baby slept peacefully under the protection of the wide, colorful beach umbrella. The warm summer breeze ruffled his silky, black hair, so like his father's. Alfred James, or A.J. as everyone called him, had the thick quilt bunched in one tiny fist, his knuckles pressed firmly against his angelic lips. Long, dark eyelashes fanned across his rosy cheeks, and when he sighed in his sleep, Laura's chest tightened with emotion. A.J. was the beautiful product of the deep and powerful love she and Dylan felt for each other.

She had insisted that the baby be named after Dylan's father, the man who changed her life by bringing her and Dylan together. Her husband had agreed, feeling that his father would have been more than pleased to know his grandson carried his name.

"Mom!" Brian shouted as he ran toward her.

She placed her index finger to her lips. "Shhhh," she cautioned. "You'll wake the baby."

"Sorry," he said in a lower tone.

Dylan collapsed on the blanket beside her, planting a quick kiss on her mouth. He tasted of sea salt and the warm, familiar maleness that never ceased to stir her.

"Look what we caught," Brian whispered.

He opened his hand and offered her a peek at the tiny, white sand crab nestled in his palm.

Laura fought the urge to recoil from the ugly crustacean and forced herself to smile. "Nice," she commented.

"Dylan helped me catch it."

"I was also the one," Dylan added softly, "who suggested Brian come and show you our find. I know how much you like the little creatures."

He sent his fingertips lightly crawling up her forearm. His touch sent shivers up her spine and she laughed, playfully slapping at his hand.

"I'm going to find some more." Brian raced toward the shore.

Dylan slid his palm across her bare midriff. His fingers had been cooled by the ocean water and felt good against her sun-heated skin.

"It's a beautiful day," he said.

She studied him a moment. "Are you missing Abbie?"

He sighed and nodded silently, his gaze turning out toward the horizon. "But it was time," he said. "She's been wanting weekend visits with her mother for months now." He swiveled his head to look at Laura. "And T.C. has really worked hard to prove herself. She's got her own place. She's supporting herself." He sighed again. "It was time."

Laura stroked his firm, tanned biceps. "You're handling this very well," she told him quietly. "You have from the beginning."

He cocked his head and murmured, "I love my daughter. I'd do anything to make her happy." Then he added, "I feel the same about Brian, and A.J., and—" he guided her down onto the blanket, planting his elbows on either side of her "—you."

His kiss was hot and moist, and Laura closed her eyes and wove her fingers through his hair. She felt his tongue trail across her lips and recognized his intimate appeal for entry. Her lips parted for him, and she reveled in the passion he could rouse in her with a simple kiss.

Disappointment washed over her when he drew back. But she had to grin at the sensuous gleam that lit his coal-black eyes.

"I love you," he said.

Those three tiny words filled her with indescribable happiness.

"I love you, too."

His index finger deliciously skimmed along the sensitive skin of her neck and he searched her gaze for a long, silent moment. "How are you doing?"

Her brow creased. "What do you mean?"

He traced the outline of her ear. "I know that you agree with my decision that Abbie should spend every other weekend with T.C. because we talked about it. But...I've never asked you how *you* feel about..." His voice trailed off, then he started again, "You came to town looking to start a day care."

"My dream." Her voice was barely a whisper.

"But what you got was a mess."

She was helpless against the tiny chuckle that

erupted from the back of her throat. "What I got," she corrected, "was joy. Paradise. Heaven."

He looked unconvinced. "I've been amazed over and over by the fact that you don't seem to be threatened by T.C. and Abbie's relationship. You've never shown the slightest resentment when I've met with T.C., or called her, or—"

Laura placed her fingertips against her husband's lips. Her smile was open and unreserved. "I don't need to feel threatened or resentful," she said. "I feel the same way about our children as you do. I only want the best for them." She reached up and cupped her palms around his strong jaw. "And besides," she added, "I know you love me. I feel so secure in the love we feel for each other that there's no room for anxiety or doubt."

She laced her fingers behind his neck and pulled him to her.

"No room at all," she breathed against his lips.

His mouth captured hers with an intensity that set her heart racing furiously. She loved this man and he loved her. And in his arms she knew that all her dreams had come true.

* * * * *

SILHOUETTE Romance™

Escape to a place where a kiss is still a kiss...
Feel the breathless connection...
Fall in love as though it were
the very first time...
Experience the power of love!

Come to where favorite authors——such as
Diana Palmer, Stella Bagwell,
Marie Ferrarella and many more——
deliver heart-warming romance and genuine
emotion, time after time after time....

Silhouette Romance——
stories straight from the heart!

Silhouette®
Where love comes alive™

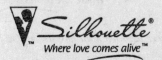